"*A Week in the Life of a Roman Ce*
century history cloaked in an arres of a Roman centurion and his young slave, Tullus. Burge's careful reconstructive work frames and fills in the story, with each chapter concluding with more detailed information about the various topics raised in that chapter (e.g., Capernaum, honor and shame, the Roman army). Yet for all its pedagogical value, the reader will be riveted by the story itself—an imaginative retelling of the backstory of a centurion who comes to Jesus for healing for his slave. Gary Burge proves to be a masterful storyteller in this engaging and fast-paced narrative. A great book for anyone interested in the New Testament and its social world."
Jeannine K. Brown, professor of New Testament, Bethel Seminary, San Diego

"I couldn't put this book down. Part historical novel and part cultural handbook, Gary Burge's *A Week in the Life of a Roman Centurion* is a delight to read. This will be a great supplemental text for my New Testament courses. Students will be so entertained they won't even realize how much they're learning!"
Mark L. Strauss, professor of New Testament, Bethel Seminary, San Diego

"Masterfully written and extensively researched, this fast-paced account invites the reader into the first-century world of the Gospels even while intriguing the reader as a good story should. In contrast to some scholars' wooden portrayals of all Jews or Romans or Syrians as the same, in this story, the characters are nuanced and come alive."
Craig Keener, F. M. and Ada Thompson Professor of Biblical Studies, Asbury Theological Seminary

"Biblical scholars are not typically known for writing historical novels, much less gripping page-turners. Gary Burge, however, has accomplished both of these feats. Fully true to the historical-cultural setting of the early first-century Roman empire, this story not only makes the New Testament world come alive but it creates one very plausible scenario of the career and family of the Capernaum centurion of Matthew 8:5-13 and Luke 7:1-10. The characters become so real that I was even tearing up at the end of Burge's story!"
Craig L. Blomberg, Distinguished Professor of New Testament, Denver Seminary

A WEEK IN THE LIFE OF A ROMAN CENTURION

•◇•

GARY M. BURGE

An imprint of InterVarsity Press
Downers Grove, Illinois

For my parents

InterVarsity Press
P.O. Box 1400, Downers Grove, IL 60515-1426
ivpress.com
email@ivpress.com

InterVarsity Press® is the book-publishing division of InterVarsity Christian Fellowship/USA®, a movement of students and faculty active on campus at hundreds of universities, colleges and schools of nursing in the United States of America, and a member movement of the International Fellowship of Evangelical Students. For information about local and regional activities, visit intervarsity.org.

Cover design: Cindy Kiple
Interior design: Beth McGill

Image: The Confession of the Centurion, illustration from "The Life of Our Lord Jesus Christ," by James Jacques Joseph Tissot / Brooklyn Museum of Art, New York. Purchased by Public Subscription / Bridgeman Images

ISBN 978-0-8308-2462-5 (print)
ISBN 978-0-8308-9773-5 (digital)

Printed in the United States of America ♾

As a member of the Green Press Initiative, InterVarsity Press is committed to protecting the environment and to the responsible use of natural resources. To learn more, visit greenpressinitiative.org.

Library of Congress Cataloging-in-Publication Data
A catalog record for this book is available from the Library of Congress.

P 20 19 18 17 16 15 14 13 12 11 10 9 8 7 6 5 4 3 2 1

Y 32 31 30 29 28 27 26 25 24 23 22 21 20 19 18 17 16 15

Contents

Characters

Albus A centurion and primus pilus of a Roman legion in north Syria. A career centurion assigned to the twelfth Roman legion called Fulminata. An old friend of Appius.

Amazon A female Roman gladiator traveling with blood-sport shows in the eastern Mediterranean.

Antipas Known as Herod Antipas, he was the son of Herod the Great. At his father's death in 4 B.C., he gained rule over western Galilee, while his brother Philip ruled eastern Galilee and portions of southern Syria. Known best for killing John the Baptist (Mk 6:14-28) and his appearance at the trial of Jesus (Lk 23:6-12). He ruled until A.D. 39.

Appius A centurion and primus pilus of a Roman legion in south Syria. Originally from Attalia in south Anatolia on the Mediterranean Sea. A career centurion assigned to the third Roman legion called Gallica (based in Raphana, Syria).

Axius A legionnaire stationed in Caesarea, striving to become a centurion. Originally from Carthage in north Africa.

Chuza A Jewish bureaucrat who owns a concession to collect taxes in the district of Capernaum. Also the financial minister of Galilee under the local rule of Herod Antipas. During this period, he lives in Sepphoris. His wife is Joanna, a secret follower of Jesus. See Luke 8:1-3.

Gaius The Arab household slave of Appius who manages Appius's villa as well as his slaves.

Livia The female slave/concubine of the centurion Appius.

Marcus Appius's personal military assistant, assigned to him in Caesarea. Originally from Sardis in west Anatolia.

Mariam The midwife of Capernaum and the wife of the only physician/healer in the village.

Maxilla A female Roman gladiator traveling with blood-sport shows in the eastern Mediterranean.

Onias The father of Tullus, an oil trader who lives in Emesa, Syria. Today this is Homs, Syria.

Pilatus Known as Pontius Pilatus (or Pontius Pilate), he was the fifth governor of Judea under Roman rule. He was responsible for the finances of the province and had at his command four or five military cohorts. Appointed by the Emperor Tiberius in A.D. 26 from the Roman upper middle class (or equestrians), his rule was severe and notorious for its violence. His murder of many Samaritans and the outrage that followed led to his ouster in A.D. 36.

Tobias The leading elder of the Jewish village of Capernaum who negotiates diplomatic connections with the Romans. He is likely a Pharisee and committed to resistance against Rome.

Tullus The slave/scribe of Appius, captured in the siege of Emesa, Syria.

1

From Emesa to Raphana

Tullus never imagined he would see a Parthian standing this close, armed and clearly intending harm. The Parthian would make fast work of him. How in the name of the gods, he wondered, had the Parthians breached the fortress of Dura-Europos?

Tullus remembered what he had learned about the Parthians. In the Roman barracks they talked about them almost every day. And the Romans hated them. They mocked them and shared endless jokes about them. Parthians were just another breed of barbarian, with an uncivilized culture and undisciplined ranks. Killing them was easy, or at least that was what the centurions told the soldiers as they drilled them daily on the fort grounds. The javelin-targeting pole in the courtyard usually wore a Parthian uniform, torn from some unfortunate victim in a recent skirmish. It was riddled with holes. Everyone knew the enemy was Parthian.

Tullus was not made for battle. He had neither the instincts nor the physique. He could have been an archer. Maybe. Archers were different from infantry, more refined, perhaps even smarter. He imagined them making mathematical calculations as they fired their arrows in careful paths through the sky. Arrows were graceful. Swords were not. But he never imagined himself as a legionnaire, who could march endlessly, carrying armor, supplies and weapons, and then at day's close begin a siege work.

Tullus was literate. And this alone saved him. The truth is, he was lucky to be alive at all.

THE PARTHIAN EMPIRE

Parthia was the first-century name for the great Persian Empire, which reached back into Old Testament times (Cyrus the Persian king liberated the Jews following the exile). The Parthians had their capitals at Ecbatana and Ctesiphon, not far from Babylon. The empire desired expansion west into Mesopotamia because of the prosperity of the Tigris and Euphrates river valleys. And yet it could go no further, due to the Roman Empire that blocked it. The desert region west of Mesopotamia (and south of the Euphrates) was called Syria. Parthia dreamed of controlling Syria. But western armies (both Greeks and Romans) always stopped them.

▪ ▪ ▪

Two years earlier Tullus had been captured during the siege of Emesa on the Orontes River in Syria, when the Emesani tribes revolted. He was not one of the Emesani—Tullus's father was from the coast, a trader in olive oil—and when the siege of Emesa was finished, Tullus was found hiding in the ruins of his school. He had heard about Roman sieges before. But nothing could have prepared him. He believed that the Romans were the true barbarians of the world. And Syria had been under Rome's control for more than seventy-five years.

As the pillaging of the town wound down, Tullus found himself tied to hundreds of other petrified young men and paraded before the Romans. Slavers who shadowed the legion were offering the officers sizable sums to take the young men away to slave markets in Antioch. The young women had already disappeared. And now, with the bartering pounding loudly in his ears, his senses dulled. Tullus was in shock. Behind him the city of his childhood lay smoldering. The smells of a burning city and the cries of the defeated would never leave his memory. He could not imagine the fate of his family—in fact, he pushed these thoughts from his mind—and now, as he stood in the hot desert sun, he listened to men from distant places putting a price on his life. He would become a laborer, a household servant, or perhaps a sex slave in a large and distant Greek city. He considered praying. But to whom? The Roman gods were obviously powerful. He knew their names. He'd grown up with them.

Just then Tullus spotted the Roman officer Appius for the first time. He was an impressive sight. A large man, likely from Rome, Appius bore the stature of an infantry commander. He walked as if he owned Emesa. His clean armor gleamed. His helmet, with its wide, feathered crown, was resting beneath his arm. His sword was still in hand. Clearly he did not like what he saw: the undisciplined looting of the town, the slavers muscling in on opportunity, and the hordes from other towns waiting to pick over what remained of Emesa when the legion departed. Emesa was prosperous, and the surrounding villages both thrived from it and resented it. Tullus recognized many of the looters as those who had been friends of his father and profited from his trade in olive oil. Here they were poised to steal what they could from Emesa.

Appius was not there for personal gain but for security: assuring Rome that its eastern flank was secure, that the Syrian

THE ROMAN ARMY

The Roman army had undergone an extensive reorganization with the rise of Augustus (or Octavian) in 27 B.C. and the growth of autocratic rule. The army became professionalized and was organized into twenty-eight "legions" that made up a fighting force of about 300,000. These were professional soldiers.

Each legion had about 5,500 men, and these were divided into ten "cohorts." Each of the cohorts from the second to the tenth mustered about five hundred men each. The legion also had various auxiliary troops, such as cavalry, scouts, horn blowers, medics, scribes and dispatch riders. These nine cohorts were then subdivided into six "centuries," each with eighty to a hundred men. One centurion led each century, along with his assistants (*principales*). Finally, each soldier belonged to an eight-man "unit" (*contubernium*): they ate together, shared a tent, sometimes shared one mule, and, when in barracks, lived in the same block.

Figure 1.1. Bust of a centurion with helmet

The tactical fighting force was made up of the legion's highly mobile ten cohorts with their staff of centurions. These were numbered and named: each bore its own standard, which was carried whenever the cohort moved.

The "first cohort" was elite. Each of its five centuries was double in size (they held 160 men, not eighty, which is why the first cohort could muster at least eight hundred). It was filled with veterans, and its centurions were the most skilled. The *primus pilus* who led it held immense prestige: he was the top centurion of the leading cohort of the entire legion.

The legion also had senior officers (*tribunes*), and above them the legion commander (the *legatus*), who often had senatorial rank and was appointed by the emperor. Often the legion had one highly honored officer, the camp prefect

Figure 1.2. A relief frieze of first-century Roman soldiers

(*praefectus castrorum*). He was an older man who had given the army a lifetime of service and had once been a primus pilus. He could lead the legion if the legatus and the senior tribunes were absent.

Senior officers enjoyed remarkable privileges. Despite an official ban on marriage, senior centurions frequently kept families at or near the legion barracks. Some had concubines and slaves. Legionary life was an enormous commitment. In the imperial era legionnaires were committed to twenty-five years of service to the army.

tribes would not challenge Roman control and, above all, that Parthia in the far east would never make its way to the Mediterranean Sea. For Appius violence was a necessary tool for bringing safety to the citizens of the empire. And therefore it was virtuous.

Appius walked up to Tullus, looked him over carefully and said, "I'll take this one."

Tullus was immediately pulled from the ranks, and the ropes holding him were loosened. Appius ordered him to follow as they walked through the gathering formations of the legion. Legionary soldiers were lodging standards in place that displayed the emperor's name. And there for the first time Tullus saw the legion's double-bull standard, lifted high above the cohort that Appius served. This was the *Legio Tertia Gallica,* the third legion, called Gallica. It had been stationed in Syria for decades. And its bull symbol was known throughout the empire. It was a frontier legion that rarely knew the comforts of a Roman city, a

LEGIO TERTIA GALLICA

Gallica (legion three) was one of twenty-eight legions operating in the first-century Roman Empire, and it was distinguished by having been founded by Julius Caesar himself in about 49 B.C. Each legion had a legionary standard and symbol, and Gallica was known as "the bull." Mark Antony had sent Gallica to the east to subdue the Parthians, who were threatening to conquer Syria. Gallica had done well and so remained, based in Syrian Raphana, south of Damascus. Sometime in the late first century Gallica was transferred to the Danube River region in the Balkans.

legion that sought out battle. It attracted a certain type of soldier or mercenary, one who liked combat. The legion's members were proud of their imago: *Taurus*, the bull. Coins represented the legion with a double bull.

Tullus followed in a daze. The landscape was familiar, but it had been overrun. Fires burned everywhere. He walked past corpses that no one planned to bury. Children over the age of five were being herded and handed over to the slavers for free. Younger children were being left behind and would likely be taken by local villagers, only to become slaves. The pungency of war and Roman arrogance were in the air. They had proven themselves again.

Tullus had his sandals and a now-filthy tunic, but that was all. Everything had been lost the instant four armed men in red tunics stormed his school and killed his teacher. His mind kept returning to the moments before the end of life as he knew it. They had been reading a comedy by Chuza Maccius Plautus in Latin, and everyone was laughing. Then their teacher read Plautus's legendary epitaph from two hundred years earlier. It was the last thing the teacher read in his life:

postquam est mortem aptus Plautus,	Since Plautus has met death
comoedia luget,	Comedy mourns,
scaena est deserta,	Deserted is the stage.
dein risus, ludus Iocusque	Then Laughter, Sport and Wit,
et numeri innumeri simul	And Music's countless numbers
omnes conlacrimarunt.	All together wept.[1]

---

[1]The text of Plautus' self-written epitaph is found in Aulus Gellius' collection of sayings "Attic Nights." In 1:24 Gellius records three epitaphs including this one from Plautus. See the Latin and English texts in the Perseus Project (http://perseus.uchicago.edu, accessed September 2014).

The Latin was difficult, but with coaching they had understood. Now laughter had indeed left his world. And Tullus wondered whether he would ever laugh again. He was ready to write his own eulogy.

Appius led Tullus to his tent, where other soldiers and centurions were standing. Tullus's stomach knotted in dread. It was a world of horses, weaponry and men constantly testing each other. And now a new and different laughter began, with legionnaires asking whether they could borrow "the boy" for the night, or did Appius have plans of his own? But Tullus noticed it again: a look that invited no levity, a look of displeasure and threat. Appius glanced at them menacingly, and almost immediately they fell silent. The boy was off-limits, and they knew it.

Appius was the primus pilus, the leading centurion of the first cohort of one of Rome's foremost legions. No centurion outranked him. Most feared him. And, yes, he had other plans for the boy.

"So what can you do?" Now seated in a beautifully crafted camp chair of carved wood and leather, Appius was peeling off his armor, drinking occasionally from a dented chalice of barley beer. He never looked up at the boy.

"Anything, Lord." Tullus stood motionless. He stared at the ground and then looked at the centurion's short sword, lying on top of the small pile of leather and bronze armor. It was a personal weapon, and its handle was intricately carved from an exotic, dark wood. Bands of bronze decorated it every few inches. He had never seen anything like it.

"I know we found you in the Greek school. Can you read?" Appius lifted the chalice and drained it. He spit some of the beer's pulp into the sand.

"I can read. And I can write. Is this your need?"

"It is my wish. I need a slave who can assist with my writing. Otherwise I will sell you and find another."

But writing would wait. Tullus soon found himself working alongside other slaves belonging to the first-cohort centurions. The first task was packing tents and provisions and loading them on mules that would follow the army on its march back to its home in Raphana.

Appius had now joined his cohort to lead it across potentially dangerous terrain. It would take them five days of following the western Syrian mountains south before they came to the oasis of Damascus. Each night was the same. They erected the camp, built fires and posted sentries on a defensive perimeter. Appius held an assembly with the fifty or so centurions from all ten cohorts. Then he would depart to meet with the legion's half-dozen tribunes and the legion prefect, an older man who himself had been primus pilus once. Meanwhile Tullus learned to cook, clean and remain invisible. He slept on the ground outside Appius's tent. And he never considered flight. Syria was filled with Roman soldiers, and the penalty for a runaway slave was death. Tullus could have stolen a sword or a lance easily. But then what would he do with it?

Raphana was Gallica's permanent camp. It was a Greek city located in a high desert, and once you stepped inside, signs of Greek culture were everywhere. Its theater, markets and temples belied its remote setting. These were like people who *wished* to be elsewhere. Tullus learned that Appius lived in the city in a villa remarkable in size and splendor. High stone walls enclosed inner courtyards and gardens, completely disguising them from the public. An aqueduct fed the city with a generous supply of water, making Raphana one of the better cities of the Syrian desert. This water supply furnished not only fountains in the public squares but also residences such as Appius's villa.

The decor of Appius's villa was carefully tended—paintings on the plastered walls within showed garden scenes and animals, fountains fed gardens that interrupted winding paths, and open-air rooms were shade cooled from the desert sun. Statues of the Greek god Apollo—Appius was a collector—occupied almost every corner. Tullus had never seen such opulence. While Tullus's own family was poor but comfortable, Appius was rich by any standard. The villa was on a small hill far enough from the markets that the smell and noise of the crowds were undetectable. A high-desert breeze blew through the villa from the west as dusk fell.

Tullus, left to himself, wandered aimlessly around the villa. He met other servants, and there were numerous hired workers who came in each morning to tend the property. One impressive household slave, a large Arab man named Gaius, was clearly in charge of everyone else, from the kitchen to the garden. He never walked but seemed to float over the pavement, his robes like ship's sails following him. And when he appeared, often by surprise, fear filled the room. His face was scarred where it once had been lacerated in a fight. Gaius's right eye seemed milky white. His stare was both intimidating and unsettling.

Tullus observed that Gaius treated him differently. Was it his youth that evoked sympathy? Tullus sensed something else, something that set Gaius ill at ease. Was it his connection to Appius? Was it his access to some of the centurion's most confidential matters? Was it his ability to write—something that even Gaius could barely manage? It seemed that Gaius directed the affairs of the estate by memory. Every contract and detail was recalled, every agreement memorized, no payment forgotten. But Gaius never appeared to put reed to paper. Could literacy intimidate? No, Tullus decided. Gaius feared something. Something connected to Tullus. And the young slave sensed it had to do with Livia.

"So you are Appius's new trophy?" were Livia's first words to

APOLLO AND DAPHNE

The Greek god Apollo and his romantic pursuit of the goddess Daphne was one of the most celebrated themes of antiquity—likely depicting the tension between seduction and chastity. After Apollo teases and offends the god Eros for his lack of military prowess, Eros shoots Apollo with a golden arrow, filling him with desire for the woodland goddess. She flees, which only further inflames Apollo's desire. (In Latin mythology, Eros is Cupid, and this is the source of romantic "arrows" today.)

Figure 1.3. Bust of Apollo, son of Zeus

Ovid was an early first-century Latin poet whose epic poem *Metamorphoses* (*Transformations*) depicts the history of the world and its major themes. In book one, he describes Apollo and Daphne. This myth drew enormous attention in the fine arts throughout Christian history and was depicted repeatedly in the Renaissance. Its most famous representation may be Bernini's marble sculpture (1625), now at the Galleria Borghese in Rome.

Tullus. Her voice was unlike any woman in his experience. It was sensual. And it drew all of his attention at once.

They were standing near the atrium fountain. She was leaning against a full-size statue of the young Apollo, almost as if she were his consort. Young, fluent in Greek, Livia was dressed in folds of embroidered white fabric that draped from her shoulders to well below her knees. Silhouetted by the bright sky, the fine fabric of her Greek tunic (a *chiton*) appeared transparent. She was intentionally alluring.

Tullus was shocked and sensed danger immediately. In Emesa a young woman would have barely looked at him, much less started a conversation. But here was a woman potentially attached to Appius—his wife? his concubine?—and Tullus knew he must tread carefully.

"A trophy?" Tullus began to plot a way to escape. He unconsciously took a step back.

"What else could you be? Another campaign, more spoils, more trophies. Perhaps you reminded Appius of Apollo himself." Livia began walking toward him. She bore the confidence of one closing in on her prey. Tullus tried to step back but couldn't move.

Fear rose in Tullus's throat. Even this conversation posed danger. He imagined Appius rounding the corner, seeing both of them, Livia laughing in the garden, and Appius drawing his own conclusions. Behind Livia, a mural covered one wall: it was Apollo, the god of music, chasing the beautiful Daphne, the goddess of the woodlands. Tullus recalled the words of the Roman poet Ovid describing her:

Enchanting still she looked–
her slender limbs bare in the breeze,
her fluttering dress blown back,
her hair behind her streaming as she ran;
and flight enhanced her grace.[2]

---

[2]Ovid's description of Daphne is found in the Latin poet's *Metamorphoses* 1.500. See the Perseus Project (http://perseus.uchicago.edu, accessed September 2014).

Tullus withdrew. He had no experience with such women, and it was clear that Livia had taken an interest in him. Tullus was young, but not so young to think that attention like this did not matter. He knew the story of Apollo—how frustrated desire could lead to profound disappointment—and that Eros's work could change the course of one's life. But he had not been struck by Eros's golden arrow yet, and he knew its dangers. Livia watched as he quickly and awkwardly retreated.

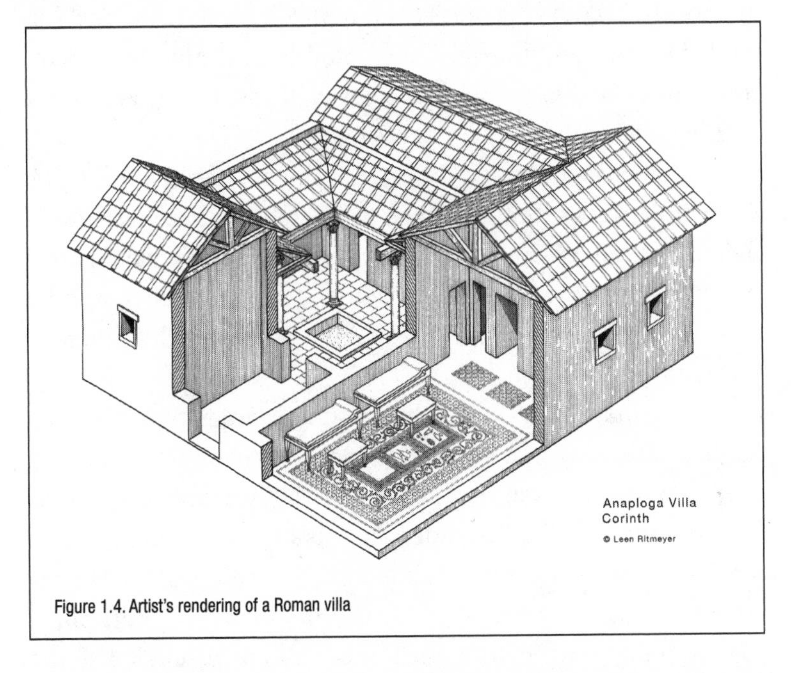

Figure 1.4. Artist's rendering of a Roman villa

Clearly life in the villa required delicate skills of diplomacy. The shadow of the tragedy in Emesa still hung over Tullus. He did not know what had happened to his family, and he could not imagine how he might find them. But a pattern eventually set in, with Tullus usually following Appius throughout the day. When the Legion Gallica was mustered, Tullus became a secretary and assistant, running to collect everything from papyrus bundles to provisions.

Drilling was the constant routine of the cohorts. These were professional soldiers, and the maintenance of their uniforms and their weapons preoccupied them. Skilled, older centurions led hundreds of young men through training in combat. Charged with the war readiness of the legion, the roving Appius watched much of the training. They rehearsed and drilled until the movement of the cohort on the field was efficiently and effortlessly coordinated. They could lock shields to deflect incoming arrows. They could dismantle and rebuild catapults in the dark. And they had endurance. They could break camp and move through the night with a practiced stealth, assaulting an enemy before they knew what had happened.

The legion maintained a camp on the perimeter of the city, and within weeks Tullus knew it intimately. He understood the defense-works of the camp—its trenches, gate signals, patrol patterns—he knew the cohort billeting arrangements, and he had begun to recognize the centurions who led their eighty-man centuries.

But the first cohort was different. It was larger, filled with the legion's most skilled men, and divided into five centuries, each made up of about 150 men. Tullus knew these five centurions best because they were under Appius's direct command and worked closely with him. Tullus often served as a courier for Appius, whose authority over the legion's soldiers was absolute. When Tullus arrived with a summons or correspondence, the centurions treated him as if he were bearing Appius's own powers. With time he became a trusted courier, returning to Appius with personal messages from the centurions. And he began to believe that this was a life he might master.

Life within the legion seemed simple enough to Tullus. Rank had its clarifying benefits, and because of it everyone knew the privileges and duties that held him. Few broke the boundaries set between officers and legionnaires. Centurions were not officers per se. They were middlemen who understood the soldier's life, for they had lived it themselves, and they could interpret it for camp officers who were generally short-term political appointments. The uniform of Gallica seemed ill-fitting on many of these aristocratic officers. And occasionally Tullus observed how centurions, who had given their lives to the legion, gave only formal respect to those above them. It took very little beer to get the centurions talking off duty in their exclusive barracks at the center of the camp. The centurions were the true engines of the legion, and they knew it. They could motivate and lead a fighting force, and they enjoyed the absolute loyalty of their men.

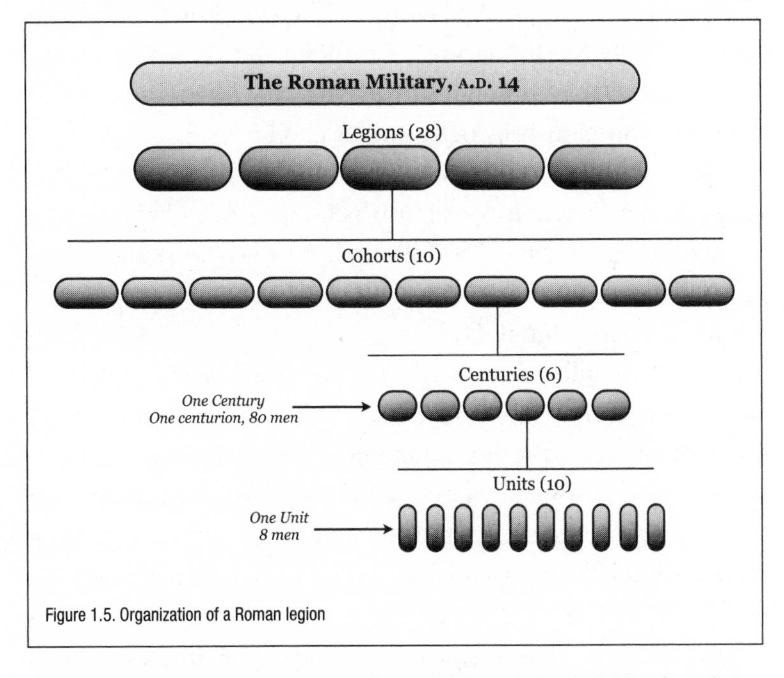

Figure 1.5. Organization of a Roman legion

But it was life in the villa that Tullus found difficult. There were no clear boundaries, or at least none that Livia wouldn't break through anyway. Rank? It was invisible, though real. No average slave spoke with Appius. Slaves who worked the estate only spoke with Gaius, who had the power to guarantee their future or ruin their lives. It was Gaius who reported to Appius, and it was Livia who seemed to distract them both.

With time Tullus settled in, while one season moved to the next. The heat of the summer would lift, the early rains would fall, and the Syrian desert would fill with flowers. And Tullus slowly learned the rhythms of the household. He could see how deeply Appius trusted Gaius. He could also see how much Appius enjoyed Livia. She was probably twenty years younger than he, and she knew how to distract him from the pressures of the legion. She was mysterious and evasive and flirtatious, all with a skill that Tullus grew to admire. And with this she won Appius's daily attention. Tullus began to think that Apollo and Daphne were not just myths for this household. In some odd way they set the roles played unconsciously by both Appius and Livia.

"You spend far too much time holding a quill." It was Livia again, in her flirtatious voice. It was her practiced habit to surprise someone, particularly Tullus when he was working on Appius's correspondence. The small scribal room at the villa was barely furnished, but it did have a couch. She reclined, her bare feet buried in pillows at the far end, and leaned statuesquely on one elbow. Clearly she was posing—Tullus could see it—aiming her seductive skills at the young man.

"Appius is an important man, and he gives me more than I can do," Tullus responded, trying hard to appear busy. Seated on a floor cushion against a wall, legs crossed and with a manuscript on his lap, he looked every bit the professional scribe.

"But a man like yourself, surely you have other interests." Livia looked at him intently. Tullus noticed the details of her face—the heavy Roman eyeliner, her dark gold earrings. The jewelry was foreign and expensive.

"I have little time for entertainment. And Gaius rarely lets me out of his sight."

"But if you were with me, Gaius wouldn't say a word." Livia slipped off one of her earrings and began playing with it. She looked from the earring to Tullus, smiling.

"I have not left this villa on my own for six months, and I would now leave with you?" Tullus felt sweat rising on his arms and neck. Suddenly the room felt close.

"Of course. Appius loves his centurions—that's what takes up his time—and he hasn't taken me to the theater once this year. You would be doing him a favor." Livia crossed her legs and laid her head back on the arm of the couch. She stared at the ceiling.

"Have you discussed this with Appius?" Tullus set down his quill. He couldn't be sure what he was feeling. He was nervous but also intrigued. He felt drawn in as toward a hot flame. Livia had his attention. And she knew it.

Livia rolled over and turned to look at him directly. With a practiced toss of her loose hair behind one shoulder, she whispered, "Of course not. Appius wouldn't care." She paused. "Trust me." The words hung in the air.

The interruption came as suddenly as Livia's entrance. It was Gaius. At the door, he clearly did not approve of what he saw. His devotion to Appius was complete, and while he didn't trust Livia, still he knew how much Appius loved her. And yet scenes like this seemed to dishonor that love. Gaius silenced his thoughts, but his posture spoke more eloquently than words as he stood motionless. Both Livia and Tullus leaned back, retreating from where they had been.

Then Gaius spoke to Tullus: "There's a courier. From Damascus. You must find Appius immediately and bring him. The courier will see Appius alone. It is urgent."

2

From Raphana to Dura-Europos

Gaius spoke as if Livia were not there. He looked firmly at Tullus, who sprang into action. Tullus, knowing Appius was not home, announced his plan to run to the centurion barracks. But Gaius pulled him into a side room, where Tullus met a man hot with perspiration and covered in dust. His uniform signaled that he was a cavalryman. The sight of the courier spoke the urgency of his message. This was not how legions communicated. This was a man on a private mission, delivering a secret to the most powerful centurion in Raphana.

Tullus and the courier left the villa and hurried through the town until they reached its outskirts. A short distance outside the city's walls, they arrived at the wooden fortifications of the Gallica camp, where sentries were posted. Tullus was recognized immediately, and the two quickly made their way into the interior of the camp, the courier now with a small scroll in hand. Within minutes they were in the centurions' quarters. Accompanied by a road-soiled man from a different legion, Tullus drew immediate attention. Word spread quickly among the soldiers. Appius was summoned at once.

Appius was a weak reader, and Tullus knew it. So when Appius arrived, Tullus broke the seal, unrolled the scroll and began to read aloud.

From Albus of Legion XII Fulminata, Primus Pilus.

To Appius of Legion III Gallica, Primus Pilus.

Honor to you in the name of Tiberius Caesar, son of the divine Augustus.

At Dura-Europos, Syria.

We have prayed and sacrificed on your behalf for many days before the gods, hoping that you would be found in good health and strength. Peace to you and your household.

Many months have passed since our last meeting in Damascus. Now I come to you in need of help. We have been sent to the far north to guard forts along the great Euphrates River. But we are extended dangerously thin. I have two cohorts in my command, and I know now with certainty that Parthian armies are moving against us. I urged the Fulminata Tribunes to send us reinforcements, but they refuse. They say we have enough. But they are mistaken. The other legions in Antioch have moved their forces into the Taurus Mountains, where tribes are threatening rebellion. They cannot come to us.

I have no one. My good friend Appius, we both know what this means. Infantry are cheap to those who do not march. The Tribunes only look to Rome and their careers.

Join us as quickly as you can. Bring what centuries you have. I am at Dura-Europos. You know the place.

Welcome my messenger Felix. He has traveled far. Send him on his way so that I may be encouraged by your word.

Pax tecum. Peace be with you.

Centurions from Gallica's first cohort surrounded Appius. These were senior centurions, each deeply trusted by the primus pilus. Appius stepped away from Tullus and calmly gave orders to his officers: they would march at first dawn. One centurion was dispatched to muster the two hundred cavalry the cohort would need. Another was sent to muster a hundred mercenary archers from Phoenicia who had been in training. Two centurions would organize the baggage train that would carry all provisions as well as medical wagons. Nearly one thousand men would soon be moving swiftly north toward central Syria. Appius assigned mappers to plot their course.

Appius would lead the first cohort and its auxiliaries north to Damascus, where they would be resupplied. Then they would pull east toward the ancient oasis of Palmyra. He predicted he would be in Dura in ten days. He would need to push the cohort, but he knew these men, and they understood their task. They lived for such assignments. They were like horses straining at their bridles, ready to leave immediately. But wiser heads knew order and planning were necessary. Impulsive armies were defeated. Disciplined armies won.

The legionnaires responded instantly. Tullus could hear the noise and chatter of excited packing and arranging. The men were readying for war. They were rushing to rescue the cohorts of Fulminata in Syria. Gallica would not permit the Parthians to destroy Rome's honor.

Appius told Tullus to follow as he strode toward the tribunes' barracks nearby. There Tullus saw, as he had before, how the Gallica tribunes deferred to their primus. He carried a gravity and strength that these lesser soldiers found unsettling. Appealing to their honor and the honor of the emperor Tiberius, he explained that this might be a great moment for Gallica as it sent its best centuries to aid one of Rome's proudest legions.

There was no discussion. Gallica would be well protected at the fortress in Raphana, since nine cohorts would remain behind. The surrounding region was quiet. Appius, his cohort and his auxiliary troops were free to go north immediately. Appius thanked them and departed at once.

It took hours for the logistical planning to be completed. The mapping was checked and rechecked by skilled Syrians who knew the desert intimately. Distances were noted. A travel itinerary was built. And the baggage train was double-checked for supplies. More than sixty mules and a dozen camels would travel with them, along with dozens of wagons. All gear was kept in a constant state of readiness for times such as this.

It was late evening when Appius returned to his villa, but everyone was awake and discussing the rumored crisis that was brewing. Gaius stood at the villa's entrance with its decorated doors open as he watched the street for Appius's return. He was worried. The movement of the legion never came except when battle was at hand. And everyone knew that many would not return alive or whole.

Appius had prepared for battle many times, and the drill was well rehearsed. He embraced Gaius in a manner unexpected by the household slave. They spoke of the concerns he had for the estate during his absence. In his private quarters Appius saw that Gaius had already assembled his armor. In the morning a legionnaire would arrive with a mule carrying Appius's tent, equipment and extra weapons.

But it was Livia that Appius was most eager to see. She stood in the darkness behind a chair piled high with the centurion's gear.

"I hate this army and what they want from you. You will leave me and never return." Livia could barely speak, her voice choking with rushes of anger and alarm. Tears flowed freely, and the stain of dark makeup scarred her tunic. She was no longer a woman

THE DECAPOLIS CITIES

When the Roman general Pompey conquered the Middle East in the seventh century B.C., he emancipated numerous Greek cities in southern Syria that had labored under Jewish rule for over one hundred years. These cities provided mercenaries to Pompey as he moved on to conquer Judea and Jerusalem. In return, Pompey committed that they would no longer live under Jewish rule, despite the building of a Jewish province (named Judea). These "ten cities" (*Decapolis* from *deca*, ten, and *polis,* city) cultivated a life quite apart from that of Judea and looked to Rome for prosperity and protection. In the Gospels we learn about some of them. The Gerasene demoniac was from Gerasa, or modern Jerash, in Jordan.

Today most of these cities are in modern Jordan, with the exception of Damascus (Syria), Hippos and Scythopolis (both in Israeli Galilee). The capital of Jordan, Amman, is the ancient Decapolis city of Philadelphia. Remains of temples, theaters, markets and prominent public buildings are rarely visited by travelers to Jordan and Syria today.

The Romans occupied the entire eastern flank of the Mediterranean, and Parthia tested Rome's defenses regularly. This explains the extreme fortification of Syria and Judea in the first century. Dura-Europos (Greek *Doura Eurōpos*) was one such outpost, perched on a two-hundred-foot hill overlooking the Euphrates, that served as an early warning for Rome. Parthians and Romans had each held it, and in times of peace it became a truly multicultural trading post. Inscriptions have been found in Greek, Latin, Aramaic, Hebrew, Syriac and Persian, among others. Today Dura-Europos is located near the Syrian village of Al-Salihiyah.

Raphana was a Greek Decapolis city that may have been the same as ancient Abila (*Abila Dekapoleos*). If this is accurate it was located about eight miles northeast of the modern Jordanian city of Irbid. Since 1980 excavations have discovered Raphana's theater, city walls and numerous temples. However, some scholars are uncertain that Raphana is ancient Abila and believe it has not yet been found.

employing her sexuality for sport. She was a woman filled with fear. Livia loved Appius both for who he was and for the security she had found in him. She knew the violence of the legion and its work. And she knew that if Appius died in battle, she would be a woman without a home, discharged from the broken household like useless pottery.

Tullus returned an hour later and made his way across the courtyard to see whether Appius's provisions were in order for the morning's departure. And there he saw them. Together, embracing each other more intimately than he'd ever imagined. And he knew that despite what he had seen in Livia, she was devoted to Appius more fully than she let on.

The morning came quickly. This was to be Tullus's first forced march, and Appius was up well before sunrise. Tullus joined him and helped strap him into his armor. Tullus himself had a uniform: a chainmail shirt over a white tunic. And he wore a belt with a short dagger that he had never used. There was no plan to place Tullus at the front lines. He was a scribe and recorder who was to be kept away from the fighting. His only assignment each day was to match Appius's pace at a distance, and in the evenings never to leave his side.

Four cavalry appeared at the villa, leading an enormous black horse armored in bronze. These men were Appius's personal guard from the cohort, and they would be with him throughout the march. Before Appius mounted he turned to Tullus, who stood nearby.

"As we march, stay with the baggage train. The medical wagons will be at the front. This is where I want you." Appius was strapping on his feathered battle helmet.

"But what if we are attacked? How shall I fight?" Tullus's voice sounded plaintive; he was looking for his place in this enormous war-fighting engine.

"You will not fight." Appius was firm and he repeated the words for effect, "*You will not fight with us.* Stay in the wagon. Stay with the physicians. I will always come and find you if I know where you are. I will not forget you." There was something in Appius's expression that Tullus had not seen before. The stern centurion was showing another side of himself.

"You belong to my *familia*. I will not lose you." Tullus had never heard him speak like this before. But he now realized he belonged to something larger than he knew. Appius clearly did not see him only as a slave.

When they arrived at the camp, the first cohort was mustered, the men fully arrayed, and every centurion from the legion—over fifty of them—was present to see them off. *Cornicines,* or horn blowers, sounded the call to movement. The cavalry pulled out in front, and Tullus saw a dozen men ride off quickly toward the horizon as scouts. They were the eyes of the cohort as it marched. Other horsemen swung wide and kept the flanks of the cohort protected. Auxiliary archers followed the main body, along with the mules and wagons. The most heavily armored century brought up the rear. Appius and his guard moved freely along the column. His was the visible strength the men needed to see. And he would know at every moment the condition and fatigue of his troops. Scouts wove their way back to the cohort at intervals, consulting with him, and the mappers were at the front with the leading centuries.

Tullus was amazed at the legion's speed. They could cover thirty-five miles in a day and then erect a defensive camp for the evening. In three days they were at Damascus. Five more days would bring them to Palmyra. Then they would strike out for the Euphrates River. Each day made Tullus more apprehensive. He had seen firsthand what happens when a legion attacks. He did not want to

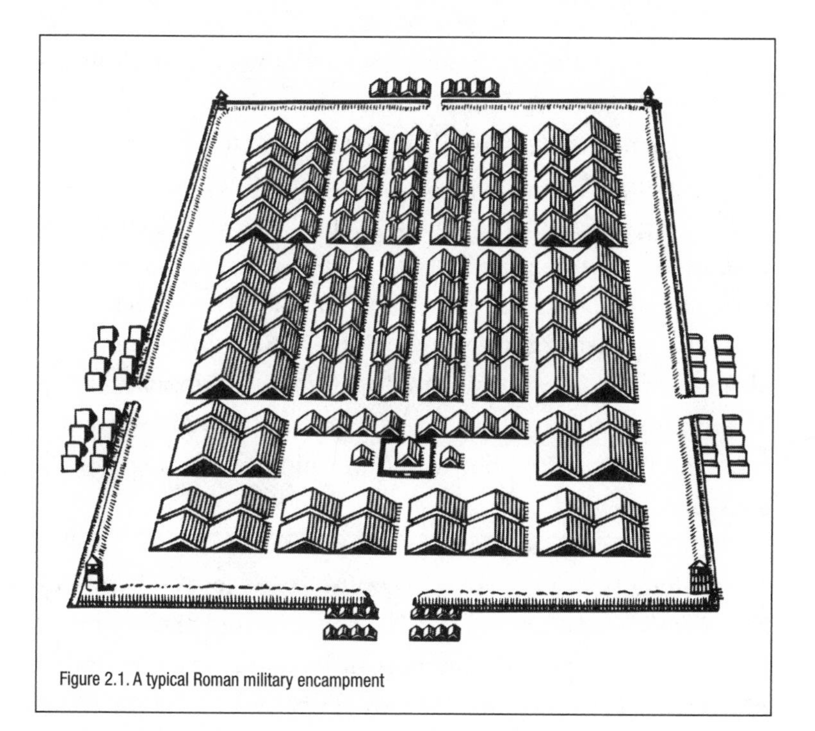

Figure 2.1. A typical Roman military encampment

see it again. But with each day the legionnaires were more determined, more confident. Their boldness grew with every milestone. Curses on the Parthian "dogs" were commonplace.

Appius had said many times that a legion in camp is a legion sick. It needed to fight. It needed to move. This cohort was being reborn with each passing day.

On the tenth day the cohort reached the Euphrates River. They had rested at the oasis of Palmyra, that ancient jewel of the Syrian desert, had resupplied at its fort, and from there had moved for days through merciless desert led by the legionary mappers of Palmyra. The risk in this was enormous, faced now with the enemies of a fierce desert heat and scarce water.

As they approached the Euphrates, the horses smelled the water first, and soon the entire cohort picked up its pace as they marched toward the huge river snaking its way through the Syrian desert. The trees and greenery hugging the river's shoulders offered shade and a welcome relief. Cavalry horses and pack animals ate hungrily in the fields and drank deeply of the Euphrates, while legionnaires filled empty goat skins stacked in the baggage train. They built a camp, and after guards surveyed their perimeter and assured themselves that they were alone, Appius permitted fires to be built and two camels to be slain for a feast. Tullus watched the revelry in amazement. Hearty breads, roast camel and beer appeared in abundance. The men told stories of past exploits and were proud to be in this moment. They knew that in the morning they would march southeast toward Dura.

Before sunrise the next day, scouts on horseback traveled south along the river's edge to confirm their location and distance from Dura, while horn blowers directed the cohort to break camp and pack the animals and wagons. On a third blast of the horn, they fell into their formations. Refreshed and eager, the men were anxious to move. Some said the horses could smell Parthians just as easily as they smelled the river.

Appius was in the front of the column when a dozen scouts rode back to him from the early morning patrol. They were

Figure 2.2. Archeological remains of a Roman military camp at Masada

nearer Dura than they thought. It was less than two hours' march. The fort had been under siege throughout the night by light Parthian infantry. But it had held fast. The scouts described their approach with care and confirmed that they had not been seen. Appius knew he had surprise on his side, and he would win the field that day.

Armor that had not been worn for days now found its owner. All of the pack animals were moved to the rear, and the auxiliary archers moved forward where Appius could use them strategically. The cavalry armed their horses with bronze breastplates and leather eye shields. Their cavalry ranks were divided in two and ran wide of the column's two flanks.

Within an hour they crested some dry hills, from which they

could see along the river's southern edge the city of Dura-Europos with its prominent Roman fortress. Some seven hundred Parthian troops were positioned near it in camps, and to Roman eyes there were few horses and little organization. The enemy was unprepared for what came next.

One wing of the cavalry ran straight for the fortress, and another wing circled to the deep southeast to cut off any Parthian retreat. Startled and overwhelmed by the size of the incoming

Figure 2.3. Remains of Dura-Europos overlooking the Euphrates River

Roman army, the Parthians fell into immediate disarray, some creating formations to meet the onslaught, others fleeing to the city where they might find cover. But they were exposed and completely unprotected from the tightly braced Roman centuries with their massive shields and spears. Tullus's wagon moved slowly toward the city as he watched in amazement. It was astounding. The Romans advanced in ominous silence. As the Parthians moved forward, they met showers of arrows that flew over the heads of the advancing cohort. Many Parthians fell before they ever met the Romans. It was like watching a wave of red and bronze flow slowly across the desert: steady, invincible, confident. It was a walled phalanx of armor and deadly precision. Soon hundreds of Roman javelins were in the air, and when they hit the Parthian infantry, the Roman cohort raised shields and ran forward with screaming war cries. The Romans took no prisoners.

Appius could see that his centurions were meeting little resistance and had no need of his direction. Centuries were moving swiftly across the plain, and the Parthians were in a full flight. The two wings of cavalry encircled the fighting, and one closed from the rear, then brutally met the Parthians as they fled.

Appius directed the baggage train to move toward the fort as he sped ahead with a dozen riders. He could see within the city that the fort had thrown open its gates and legionnaires from Legion Fulminata were running out. They met the incoming Gallica troops and immediately set about pursuing the Parthians who had taken cover in the city.

The medical wagons arrived, and Tullus dismounted gladly. His worst fears had not been realized. Their mission had been a success. Dura had been saved, and the reinforcements would eventually press the Parthians to retreat further to the east. The bottled tension that Tullus had held for hours now evaporated.

Fulminata's primus, Albus, embraced Appius in the main courtyard of the fort as more Gallica soldiers poured through the gates. Tullus followed closely and could see not only an old friendship but also the deep respect Albus and Appius had for each other. Both had risen to the highest ranks of their legions. Both had full and promising careers within the empire.

Tullus felt relieved. Appius was peeling off his heavy armor, and his personal guards were holding it as salutes and congratulations were in the air. Skirmishes were still under way around

THE EUPHRATES RIVER

The Euphrates was one of the most important rivers in antiquity. It begins in eastern Anatolia (Turkey), flows south toward Syria, and then heads southeast in a curving arch that leads to Mesopotamia, about two thousand miles. Near its end it joins the Tigris River, and this floods a vast delta that pours into the Persian Gulf. Today it moves through Turkey, Syria and Iraq.

The river served as a caravan corridor across the deserts and was the route used by Abraham as he traveled from Mesopotamia to Canaan. But it was also a highway for armies moving between Egypt and Mesopotamia, and in the Roman era it was the one route the Persians exploited to press west toward Rome.

Ordinarily travel would follow the river to the enormous market city of Aleppo, Syria. From here caravans could move southwest into central Syria, Antioch and Lebanon.

Figure 2.4. Temple of Bel at Palmyra

> The journey west could be shortened by leaving the Euphrates at modern Deir ez-Zor and moving due west to the oasis of Palmyra (Hebrew *Tadmor*; Arabic *Tadmur*). From here a caravan could move directly to Damascus. In our story Appius is eager to move north and arrive at Dura as quickly as possible. Therefore his mappers build a Damascus/Palmyra route and then go directly for the Euphrates.

the city, and sounds of clashes could be heard. But they were quickly diminishing. All was well.

Tullus decided to explore the fort to see how life was lived on the very fringe of the empire. From a rampart he wandered to a guard tower overlooking the Euphrates River winding into the distance. The Euphrates was unlike anything he had seen before: it was powerful and like a narrow, moving sea that snaked through the desert. Eventually it made its way to Babylon and places he'd only dreamed about. Below he could see how the city had built itself up against the fort's strong walls. There were two-story buildings, their roofs used for sleeping, built so near the top of the rampart that he could imagine climbing down on them.

From the tower Tullus found a staircase that led inside what appeared to be quarters for the lookouts manning the ramparts. The walls were lined with souvenirs from past Parthian conflicts: knives, swords and tunics, each bearing the distinctive patterns of Persian artistry. Arrows, piled in enormous mounds or stacked in boxes, were the chief tools of the guards who mounted the walls.

Tullus thought he was alone. And when he heard steps, he assumed it was a Roman guard still holding his post. But he was wrong.

The Parthian infantryman stared at him and stepped from the shadows. Tullus looked closely and could see the man was injured. His left arm hung limp and was bleeding profusely from the shoulder. The sleeve of his chainmail was sliced open, and blood clotted the metal rings and ran to his hand and off his fingers. In his right hand he held an enormous sword whose tip was resting on the stone floor. The Persian was breathing heavily and had no intention of letting Tullus leave and betray his whereabouts.

Tullus tried to step away, but he felt paralyzed. His body simply would not move. His feet felt leaden, and he could not keep from staring at the Parthian, whose face formed the hardened look of a soldier direct from the battle field.

Tullus heard the tip of the blade ring against stone as the Parthian hoisted it from the floor. He lifted the heavy sword slowly across his chest and swung it explosively at Tullus. The scribe heaved back and heard the air scream as the sword whipped past him and crashed into a stand of arrows on the wall. Wood splinters flew from dozens of arrows cut in half. This failure enraged the man, and he began to advance on Tullus, who now found his senses and dodged another blow. Tullus remembered his knife, but when he pulled it from its sheath, its size seemed ludicrous. The Parthian grinned and kept advancing as Tullus kept moving backward cautiously. It was cat and mouse as the wounded warrior tried to corner the scribe but found himself bogged down by the weight of his armor and severity of his injury.

Then Tullus made a mistake he would never forget. Afraid to take his eyes off the Parthian, he could not see behind himself and fell, crashing into a wood table. The Parthian closed quickly and brought the sword straight down on him. Tullus dodged and slid under the upset table while the sword crashed and ripped through timber. With the protection of the table gone, Tullus knew this was the end.

But at that moment Tullus heard his name called. At first it had been muted and distant, and then in the room. It was the one voice that ensured his safety.

"Tullus! By the gods, where are you?" It was Appius. And Albus was with him.

Tullus screamed from the floor, and the Parthian quickly turned. He could finish the boy or prepare to deal with the centurions. Deciding he had time to do both, he returned to the broken table and prepared to deliver a final, slashing blow.

All Tullus heard was the swish of a Roman short-sword as it spun through the air at a speed Tullus could not comprehend. It hit the Parthian squarely in the back, cutting through his chainmail and throwing him forward. He crashed into the table's fragments, and his huge sword dropped near Tullus, now laying prone on the floor, paralyzed in fear. The Parthian's shocked and deadened eyes stared at him, his blood flowing freely. Tullus realized that the man's blood was spreading across the floor and beneath him. It was on Tullus's hands, and this only increased the terror of the moment.

"Tullus, are you harmed? Call out to me!" Appius ran quickly across the littered tower floor, stopped to check the Parthian, and then lifted Tullus from the debris. Parthian blood covered the boy's tunic. Panic was in his eyes.

Albus screamed when he saw the second Parthian in the shadows, and quickly Appius's personal guards rushed into the room to give aid. Everyone froze. The Parthian was an archer. He had drawn an arrow onto his taut bow and was aiming it directly at Appius, who was embracing the boy and checking for wounds. Albus and the four legionnaires spread out and prepared to rush the man. Then Albus saw his worst nightmare.

Appius was uncovered—his armor was gone—and only a linen tunic and a leather vest stood between him and the Parthian. Appius's back was to the archer, and he glanced back only seconds before he heard the bowstring snap.

The arrow flew expertly across the room, and, as if in slow motion, the Romans watched it hit Appius's left shoulder and sink deeply.

3

From Dura-Europos to Raphana

•◇•

For days after the battle at Dura, Appius slipped in and out of consciousness. The battlefield physicians cut away the greater length of the arrow, but feared what would happen if they attempted to pull it out or push it through. The bleeding might be unstoppable. Soon a fever swept over Appius, and his breathing became labored. Sweat poured from his body. The physicians carefully washed the wound with vinegar and applied a poultice of herbs. The pungent smell of burning incense disinfected the air of malignant diseases and spirits hovering about. And they began to bleed the centurion, confident that cutting and draining blood would release the heat that was building in his body.

Appius's only hope was in Damascus, where there was a major healing center. People said that the god Asclepius had appeared there many times and that countless people were made well. Physicians with great skill also worked in the temple, and they would know what to do. But Appius must be taken immediately.

Two medical wagons and twenty horsemen, including Appius's own guard, departed at once for the long trip west. And as the wagon wheels bumped, jolted and thudded over the road, Appius was delirious, doped by the opium the physicians administered. Without the cohort they could move swiftly, and they arrived in Palmyra in short order. At the Roman fort they were able to change their animals and press on to Damascus. But as each day dawned, the physicians sounded less and less hopeful. Tullus never left Appius's side. This centurion had saved him in Dura from certain death. And now their bond seemed unbreakable. Tullus felt affection for Appius that he had never felt before. It was a new feeling, one he had not even felt for his own father. In a few days they had done much together. And the shared fight in the guard tower connected them in a manner he could not describe. Yes, there was a bond. And Tullus did not know what to do with it. He simply sat in the wagon with his hand on Appius's arm and prayed that Asclepius would have mercy on them.

Damascus was a Greek city—one of the distinguished Decapolis cities—and there one could find anything available in the great cities of the Mediterranean world.

The Asclepeion, or Temple of Healing, was located in the markets, and while it was smaller than those in cities like Ephesus or Pergamum, it had physicians who had trained at the best Asclepieia of the Roman world.

The arrival of so many Roman soldiers carrying one of their own immediately brought the attention of the priests and healers. Tullus gave money to the priests, who agreed to make sacrifices on behalf of Appius, who was carried on a stretcher to an examining table. When the healers had stripped off Appius's clothes and removed his bandages, the ugliness of the wound became clear. It had festered and blackened, and the physicians shared looks that were not promising.

"We must cut him immediately. And the damage will be

ASCLEPIUS

Asclepius was a Greek god who lived within the pantheons of both Greek and Roman religions. The son of Apollo, he evolved to become the god of healing and recovery, and his children followed in the same line (among them Hygieia and Panacea). The extent of his work, however, was limited by the gods: he could heal but was not to raise the dead. In some mythologies, when he presumed to raise the dead, he was killed (in one case by Zeus) for his presumption.

His primary healing center was at Epidaurus in Greece, but other healing temples, called *Asclepieia*, were throughout the Mediterranean. The island of Kos, for instance, had an enormous *Asclepeion*, and there the famed Hippocrates began his medical career. Within the temples, the wounded and sick would lay, hoping for visions of the god who could

Figure 3.1. Terra cotta body parts used as votive offerings and prayers for healing in an Asclepeion at Corinth

direct the path of their healing. In the healing rituals, nonvenomous snakes were common—they appear in numerous murals and reliefs. This explains the symbol of Asclepius: a serpent wrapped around a rod (a symbol used even today in medicine).

great." The leading surgeon was a man of about fifty who understood the risks of operating on a Roman centurion. He might save the man. But he might also kill him.

"And if he dies, it will be a course already set by the gods." The surgeon looked at the many armed men standing nearby and sought some acknowledgement. He found none. Then he lifted a satchel filled with blades and instruments. Some looked old and well used. But this inspired confidence among the observers, for these tools had been used successfully before and would bring success again. This man was no novice to the healing arts.

Tullus watched as Appius's powerful form was laid face down on the stone table. He was delirious and so could not be given more opium. Priests joined the physicians and immediately began singing chants to Asclepius. They burned incense, sprinkled holy water and waved scented leaves over him as the surgeon began to dig out the arrow. Appius moaned, then quickly and quietly passed out. Within minutes the arrow was removed, but the jagged gash in his back was sickening. Tullus could see bone beneath the bleeding and torn muscle. The surgeons closed the wound with sutures of sheep gut. Then they packed it with ground garlic, held in place with linen wrappings that wound around his shoulder and chest.

"Now we are done. And if he lives, it will be thanks to the hands of the gods. The wound was deep and the wreckage great.

BLOOD AND MEDICINE

Roman medicine made numerous advances in understanding the human body, and this led to sophisticated surgical techniques that amaze us today. Without sedatives they operated frequently on virtually every part of the body. Nevertheless, from the Greeks (and particularly Hippolytus) the Romans had inherited the theoretical idea of the four humors. This idea argued that equilibrium was what made health and that imbalance among heat, cold, wet and dry contributed to illness.

Thus a fever (which was viewed as an illness itself) was an overheating of the blood, and its best remedy was to bleed the patient (called bloodletting) to reduce his or her blood volume. The model for this, they believed, could be found in women, whose monthly menstruation relieved the body of impurities. The practice of medical bloodletting continued for over two thousand years and only ended in the nineteenth century.

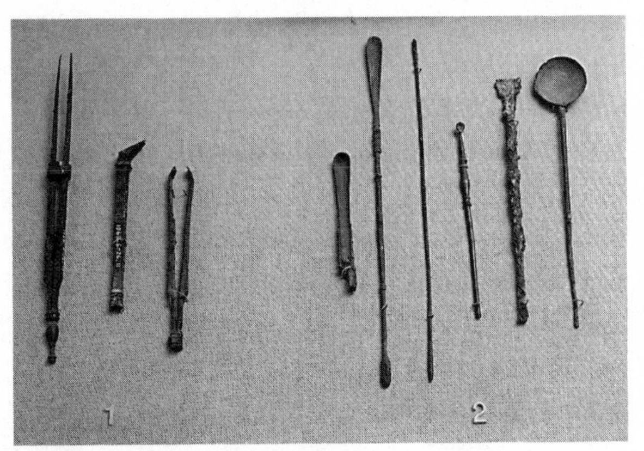

Figure 3.2. Medical and surgery instruments

This man will not return to the battlefield." The surgeon looked around the room. The other soldiers were prepared for the severe diagnosis. But not this last sentence. This was a death sentence that exceeded anything the Parthian arrow delivered.

"But surely there is a chance." Tullus spoke up plaintively and uttered the words that were on the mind of every uniformed man at the table. "Appius is strong. He will heal. He only needs time."

"I have seen hundreds of battle wounds smaller than this and with poorer results." The surgeon knew he was hearing the language of wishful hope, and this late in his career he refused to indulge it. "His arm will be useless, and if the wound does not take his life it has certainly ruined his body." This was uttered with such authority that no one refuted it.

But Dura was not a real battle, Tullus thought. *So how could this happen? How could the gods fail us? If only I had not gone off on my own. If only Appius had been armored. If only we had never gone to that useless city.*

For Tullus this tragedy evoked memories of other recent violent events. A life that centered on Raphana, its markets, its temples and the villa, was slipping away. Tullus knew it. The hope of a peaceful and routine life in the legion had been misplaced. The legion did not live to reside in a camp. It was a war machine. And death followed wherever it went. Tullus's innocence and his faith in life were slipping from his fingers. Appius and his party remained in the Damascus temple of Asclepius for a week. And when it was clear that Appius was holding on, they decided to travel south to Raphana. There were days when Appius appeared drugged and unresponsive. Other days he was clearly awake. But even then his eyes were glassy, his face lifeless. Tullus worried that Appius was departing, perhaps as good as gone. As the wagon plodded slowly south, it felt like a funeral caravan bearing a man who was no more than a shell of what he had been only days before. *The Parthians won,* Tullus thought. *Or perhaps their gods won.* Their cruelty was as familiar as their mercy. And now he was seeing nothing but cruelty.

It was nearly evening when the wagons bypassed the Roman camp of Raphana and rolled directly to Appius's villa. A courier was sent to summons the legion physicians while everyone worked to unload Appius and his gear.

Gaius was the first to emerge from the villa gates, and he immediately assessed the situation. Shouting orders to other slaves gathered on the street, within minutes he had even the legionnaires attending Appius following his instructions.

"Tell me what happened." Gaius had found Tullus near the wagon, preparing to assist in lowering Appius's stretcher to the ground.

Taking Gaius aside, Tullus spoke to him. "It was an arrow—in the fight at Dura-Europos—and the surgeons in Damascus worked on him. But he is broken, Gaius, and few believe he will return to us as he left." Tullus looked tired and dismayed. He stared at the chief servant, looking for hope or reassurance, but found none.

"We will do what we can. Make sure you carry him gently, and bring him to his room where he can be washed and dressed. You have the smell of the road on you."

As they entered the villa atrium, Gaius stopped the procession when he saw Livia biting her fist, holding back a scream. Heedless of the courtyard filled with unfamiliar soldiers, decorum meant nothing as she saw the limp and lifeless body of Appius before her. Her eyes were filled with fear, and tears flowed as she looked from Appius to Gaius and tried to gain a measure of what all this meant.

"Is he dead?" She could barely say it. Livia stepped closer and fell to her knees on the cold tile floor, bringing her hand to Appius's face. He was not dead—she could see that. But he was suffering, and his strength—the strength and fearlessness she had come to rely on—was not on this crude litter. Suddenly she felt alone, adrift, afraid.

Tullus knelt beside her and whispered. "The physicians did all they could for him. He is in the hands of the gods. But he wanted to come home. In the last three days he has repeatedly said your name in his delirium. He misses you, Livia. And if this is his last place to rest, he will do so with you."

Livia fell into Tullus's shoulder and began to cry, for Appius and for herself.

"There is no mercy in this life. Hope comes to us and is snatched away. This is unfair! Unfair! My life—our life—is finished!"

Tullus held her as the soldiers followed Gaius and carried the litter to the centurion's private quarters. There Appius was carefully lifted onto his bed, and the men retreated.

"Bring me pumice and hot water. We will wash him. And bring me olive oil with rosemary. We must welcome Appius home." Gaius dismissed everyone except Livia and Tullus, who were as fixed as statues. They removed Appius's clothes. They washed him with water and pumice and then massaged him with aromatic oil. Then, now dressed in a white tunic, Appius was left to sleep.

Visitors from the legion came to the villa the next day. But Appius was not ready to see them. He could speak, but his voice was not strong. The tribunes were the first to arrive, and the senior centurions who knew Appius well followed them. The legion had lost one of its most important men, and now critical decisions had to be made about leadership, the future and the welfare of the legion itself. Casualties were a part of legionary life. Everyone knew that. But rarely did someone become a casualty who was so well known, so admired by so many.

Appius had not lain in a bed for so many days in his entire life.

BATHING

Crude soap (mixing animal fat—tallow—and an alkali, often ash) had been in use since almost 1500 B.C. However, it was rarely used for personal hygiene. It was used to clean textiles, as a topical medicine for skin disorders and as a cosmetic ointment for the hair. The ancients did not understand germs, and the connection between hygiene and health would not appear until the late Roman period when soap use for cleaning the body became common. Romans preferred washing in water, using a soft pumice or sand. This was followed by scented oils that were scraped off with a curved metal instrument called a *strigil*.

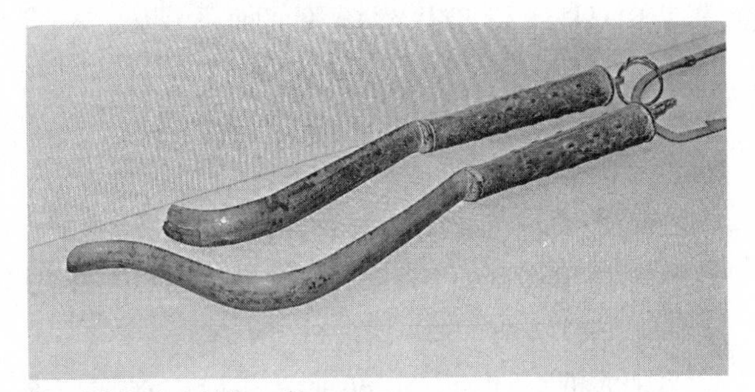

Figure 3.3. A pair of strigils, or skin scrapers

Gaius brought him everything he needed. Livia walked in and out of his room compulsively and nervously, setting Appius on edge. She wanted him to talk, to reassure her that he would be fine. But Appius remained silent, staring at the ceiling and counting his heartbeats as they throbbed from his shoulder.

He did not feel fortunate to be alive. He felt angry to be wounded.

And as his strength returned, his anger grew. His left arm was useless. He could only manage minor movement, though his hand was capable. But Appius could not lift his arm much above his chest. Its strength was gone, and efforts to press it into service only brought crushing pain. And this fed the anger brewing in his mind.

His only respite from the pain was the opium the physicians brought him daily. This slipped him into a haze of bliss and sleepiness. But even with this relief and sleep, his attitude toward Gaius and Livia and everyone in the household became unpredictable.

"The opium has helped you heal." The physicians were attending him one morning as he sat in the sunny atrium. "But it is time to end this. You cannot live your entire life in oblivion.

OPIUM

The use of opium for injury was a common therapy. Opium's cultivation extends back to the Babylonian era and possibly earlier. The poppy plant (which exudes a latex substance containing morphine) had such immediate and powerful effects on a patient's well-being (although short-lived) that many saw it as a temporary healing. Many of the Greek gods were sculpted holding these poppies and thus showing their gift to humanity. In particular, Apollo often held poppies, but they were also common in statues of the Greek god Hypnos (sleep; *Somnus* in Latin) and his twin Thanatos (death; *Thanatus* in Latin).

The god Hypnos has been tending you long enough. You must get up and return to life as best you can." The physicians knew this news would not please Appius, so this day a senior tribune who was watching him stood conspicuously with them.

"Then get out—all of you!" Appius yelled. "I know what I need.

I know what has happened to me. And you cannot tell me how I will repair myself." He tried standing but even then felt a weakness wash over him. Was it the residual opium? Was it the injury? It did not matter. He could sense the soldiers distancing themselves from him, not recognizing him for who he was. He had enjoyed enormous respect for years. And now he was sensing their pity. Rage boiled and surged inside him. It felt uncontrollable.

"We need to think about the legion and your cohort, Appius." The tribune was standing straighter, projecting strength for what he knew he had to say. "Your cohort returned this week from the north, and the centurions are already talking about what to do if you fail to return." The tribune stared at him and waited for another explosion. But it didn't come. Appius simply gazed at him without saying a word. Then Appius's soul descended to a place it had never been before.

"So I am no use to the legion." He slumped in his weakness and now dejection. A statue of Apollo, brimming with youth and virility, towered over him. The contrast was unmistakable.

"I did not say that. I simply say that we need to think about the future."

"Then I will return to Gallica and the cohort and resume my service to the emperor."

"How do you imagine that, Appius? You are too weak to even stand before us. And your arm—look at your arm. You could not even carry a battle shield, much less enter into fighting. Things have changed, Appius."

"I will challenge any centurion who dares take my place."

"Challenge with what? You cannot even dress yourself. You cannot even wear the weight of your own armor. Can you ride? Can you haul your pack and javelin as every man does? You cannot." The tribune had grown intense. This was an argument he had rehearsed. Perhaps he had used it before.

THE GLADIUS AND SCUTUM

The *gladius* (named after the gladiolus flower, with its sword-shaped leaves) was the Roman soldier's preferred weapon in infantry combat. It was a short, two-edged sword used for stabbing and thrusting when enemy lines engaged in combat. Its handle and hilt were personally built for its owner, and it was used with a large rectangular shield with a pronounced steel boss at the center (a *scutum*). The infantryman would hit his opponent with the center of the shield and then produce the gladius with an upward thrust in close quarters as his enemy regained his balance. Roman sources describe the gladius and the scutum as accounting for the successes of the Roman infantry.

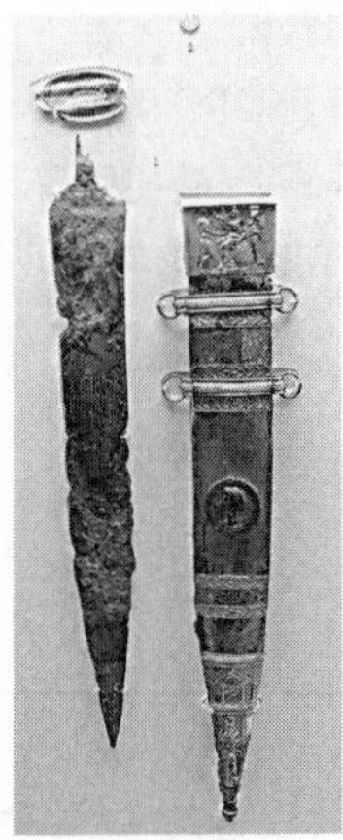

Figure 3.4. Roman sword and scabbard

Figure 3.5. Bas-relief of Roman shields

"And you?" Appius growled, "Can you march with the legions? You who barely knows how to raise a sword? You who cannot build a tent or a siege-work?" Appius stood up holding firmly to the back of a chair. He challenged the tribune to his face and tried to disguise his unsteadiness. "I could end your life in a moment with just a gladius."

"Sit down and shut up. This is not the Appius I know. This is not the man who led our legions across deserts to great honors in Syria. You are broken, Appius. And it remains to be seen whether your breaking is in your arm or in your heart. We must leave. You may not return to the legion until we speak again. Our physicians will visit you every day and report to us on your progress."

"So I am of no use."

"And do not ever threaten me with a gladius again. I will make no word of it with the others. And this will be true of all who stand here." The tribune stared at the physicians. "You are broken, primus pilus. Repair yourself and return to us. But do not return until you are whole."

Led by Gaius, the physicians and the tribune walked to the gate. When the doors shut, silence closed in on the atrium. In Appius's mind, the walls of the villa had become a prison, not an infirmary. All had been lost.

Appius began drinking not many days later. It was a combination of self-pity and medication, for when he could barely feel his head it seemed that the pain in his shoulder receded. And he cared less about the consequences of what was happening around him. Gaius supplied him with all the wine he wanted. The slave felt no ability to resist Appius. He was a slave, after all, and as the days unfolded, his own life seemed to lose the respect and honor he had once enjoyed. In the markets everyone knew why he was buying countless jars of wine. And Gaius's friends began to pity his household, his master, his life.

It was Livia and Tullus, together united, who often tried to intervene. Late one morning Appius was reclining on pillows in the dining room. It had become his usual posture. Angry, drowsy and pitiful, the great warrior had shrunk to a shell of what he once was.

"Appius, the physicians will be here shortly." Livia missed the relationship she had known only weeks earlier, before the debacle of Dura-Europos. She had said farewell to a lover, and now she had a patient. And with it she could sense Appius's affections for her flowing away.

Figure 3.6. Statue showing a Roman woman's garment of the period

"And when they come, they cannot see you like this." Livia sat next to him on the floor on cushions. She had taken to wearing her older linen tunics. This one was frayed and colorless. When she looked in the mirror, she barely recognized the person looking back at her. Appius had pulled her into his darkness as well.

Tullus was cleaning the room and stopped to listen, knowing that such conversations had failed many times before. But this day was to prove different than all the rest.

"The tribunes will hear of it, and the legion will be finished with you. Appius, you must hear me. Without the legion, where will you be? *Where will we be?* This entire household will end. And you will be a man without a life." Livia's voice carried desperation, not love, in its words. Appius sensed it.

"And am I not such a man now?" Appius slurred. "The gods have robbed me of my strength, and in their delight they have robbed me of my life." Appius was looking directly at her. His tone showed interest but barely any respect. "My fate has already overtaken me. I am without a *place* because I am broken. And broken things have no value. *I have no life.*"

"At least there is no life here, living on the floor. Living like an animal. Finding your only hope in this . . . this wine that takes you away from yourself and us."

"It is all I have."

"You have me. You have us." Here she looked at Tullus and reclaimed the deep love she had held for Appius for so long. "Appius, hear me clearly. *I will not lose you*! I will stay at your side until you heal."

Gaius interrupted. The physicians from the legion had arrived for their daily visit, but now the senior tribune was with them. What once was a demeanor of sympathy had changed to something colder, impatient and official.

Tullus recognized the dreadful scene unfolding and backed silently into a corner. Appius was lying prone on large floor cushions, with Livia at his side. He reeked of wine and soiled clothing. Livia sat beside him, while the physicians and the tribune stood over them in their best attire. The contrast of their uniforms—gleaming leather, white and red linen, and brass—stood in sharp contrast to the shameful scene on the floor.

Appius did not try to stand or sit up. Livia stood at once and stepped away from the men. Seeing Tullus, she quietly moved into the corner next to him. They knew they should leave, but they couldn't.

"Primus pilus, how do you fare?" The tribune was distant. Official. There was little warmth in the question.

"Look at me and judge for yourself." Appius rose on his right elbow and regained a measure of composure. "What the physicians say is true. My arm is useless, and I no longer can stand in battle." Here he lifted his left arm level with his chest and let it drop to his side. "I can lift a spoon but not a sword. I am broken."

The tribune drew in closer, knelt on one knee, and spoke slowly to him. "Primus Appius, we have known each other for many years. You have saved our lives and the honor of our legion many times. And for this we are grateful. Your strength has always made us strong." The tribune placed his hand on Appius's shoulder.

Appius drew himself up, knowing that this was the beginning of something he did not want to hear.

"The senior tribunes have spoken. And decided. And I speak for them." There was silence.

"We have chosen another primus from your cohort—Andronicus of Cilicia—your first assistant. We know you trust him, and it is to him the legion now looks for strength." The tribune picked up an overturned chalice, smelled its contents, and set it upright next to Appius. He watched Appius's face carefully.

"And what will become of me?" Appius withheld his anger. He had been preparing for this hour.

"We have spoken to the governor of Judea in Caesarea on the coast. We urged him to consider who you are, what you have done. And because of his long respect for Legion Gallica, he has heard us. He is welcoming you to his barracks in Caesarea."

"Caesarea?"

"Gallica is a frontier legion, Appius. We move, we fight, we patrol. You know this. Caesarea needs men of experience that will help rule a province. They will expect you within the month."

"I must do this?"

"Your other choice is to leave our service. But I urge you not to do so. Take up your household, leave this place, and remember that Gallica will always be your legion. But for now you must serve the emperor and Gallica away from us."

The tribune seemed to move in yet closer. "Appius, you *are* broken. And in ways that you cannot even see." He looked at the empty chalice. "You need to begin again, even though you are broken. Go to Caesarea. Take this introduction with you." He handed Appius a scroll sealed with the Gallica wax stamp. "We will provide all you need in wagons and escort. Already men in your cohort are asking to ride with you, to see you to the coast."

Appius looked at the tribune and the physicians who were nodding in agreement. He glanced at Livia, who was holding her breath, hoping he would agree. Tullus knew he would.

"Then I go."

Appius sat up. He gained his feet and stood firmly in a manner no one in the room had seen since before his injury.

"I will depart at the close of the week."

4

From Raphana to Caesarea

•◈•

When Appius stepped in front of his cohort for the last time, the men were arrayed in their finest uniforms, standing at ranks, with their imperial standard held high. Dozens of other centurions from throughout the legion were present as well. The new primus pilus, Andronicus, had declined to take his post and joined the ranks with the other legionnaires. For this morning, Appius was the Gallica primus, and all the soldiers of the first cohort desired to honor him.

The tribunes addressed the cohort, announcing the decision that had been reached just a week earlier. But most had already heard its rumor. And the few who had not heard expressed shock that Appius would not return.

"Appius will always be one with us," the senior tribune concluded. "He travels to Judea to serve the governor, and there he will bring honor to Gallica, just as he has always done. Andronicus of Cilicia will now lead. And you know his worth. We know that Andronicus has become what Appius has made him." Nods of approval could be seen in every rank. The rattle of swords hitting shields echoed from the ranks as hundreds of men made themselves heard. Many looked to Andronicus, who was giving his full agreement.

"I give you Primus Pilus Appius of Attalia."

This was the first time Appius had worn his full uniform since Dura-Europos. Gaius had cleaned it thoroughly, and Tullus had helped him dress. Tullus had learned neither to favor the arm nor speak of it, but to work around it wordlessly. Carefully. As if nothing were amiss.

Appius knew these men well. They had marched and camped together for years. They had fought in many battles. Most of the centurions had been his friends for almost twenty years. There was a bond here, a bond known only by men who had shared missions together. And as Tullus looked on from the edge of the formation, he envied what he saw. These men shared a purpose, a life and, above all, trust. They knew where they belonged and to whom they belonged. And that belonging was for life. Appius spoke:

> Brothers of Gallica. My time to leave you has come.
>
> I have sacrificed to the gods on your behalf. And I have prayed to Apollo that he will prosper you with success just as he has done throughout these years.
>
> Gallica is strong because you love honor more than you fear death. It is strong because you would rather die than fail to conquer. You love the taste of honor more than life itself. And so the gods have honored you in all things.
>
> Be resolute in battle and disciplined in training. The wise man prepares for war while he lives in peace. How you train will determine how you conquer. As our poets have said, "He conquers who first conquers himself." Train your mind before your arm. Discipline your passions before you discipline your sword. Take care of your sword, and your sword will take care of you. Trust the man who stands next

to you, for it is with him you live or die. And trust the centurions whom the gods have placed over you, because it is their wisdom that will bring you success.

I depart now for Caesarea. But I shall not forget. I shall not forget our victories at Damascus and Pella. Or when we brought the tribes of Emesa to order. I shall not forget the cheer of Legion Fulminata and their Primus Albus when we saved them at Dura from the Parthian foe. Parthia does not merely fear Rome. *They fear Gallica, and so they should.*

Appius paused, and soon he could hear a swell of clamoring swords against shields rise once more from the ranks, punctuated by the rumbling shouts of the legionnaires.

Remember that the divine Julius Caesar is your patron. He watches Gallica from the heavens and can send blessing or curse upon us in any year. Look to the stars, Gallica. These are the gods who watch us. They cheer our victories. They protect and strengthen us against the barbarian enemy. Without them we are nothing.

Farewell. I am stricken, but I am strong. Fear has not seized my limb, though the Parthian arrow has. But know this. One Roman arm can best a forest of Parthian swords. And so if you meet the Parthian enemy again, complete my joy by returning to these barbarians gifts I could not give at Dura. Repair my honor with the boldest revenge.

Peace be with you.

With this, Appius saluted the tribunes, nodded to the centurions who were gathered in the field and raised his drawn gladius high above the cohort as each man raised his gladius in response. Appius turned, resheathed his sword and began to walk away. Tullus considered following him immediately, but he waited and

HONOR AND SHAME

Farewell speeches were a common genre within Roman society. Appius's speech is a composite of other ancient speeches given during this period. Notice how often he refers to honor. Within Roman society (and other societies at this time) the loss, preservation and accumulation of honor were foremost on the mind of most people. Personal honor was important, but how one contributed to corporate honor (the family, the clan—in this case, the legion) was critical. Honor was reflected and shared—few persons saw themselves as pure individuals—and so one could shame one's community as well as escalate its honor.

Honor was like a bank deposit, with many people holding a debit card. Everyone could see who was contributing richly and who was depleting the account foolishly. And if honor was lost in a manner one could not control (such as Appius's injury and defeat by a Parthian), the group (or the legion) would feel a duty to reclaim that lost honor with revenge. That act would enhance Appius's honor, but as an act of honorable revenge would also increase Gallica's honor. The man who killed a Parthian archer *in Appius's name* would be honored above all.

let the primus exit the fort alone, silently and with dignity.

Four wagons were loaded and parked outside Appius's villa early the next morning. Appius's personal battle guard was awarded the privilege of riding with him to Caesarea. They brought his horse, fully groomed and dressed. And not long after sunrise, with a half-dozen household slaves clambering into the last wagon, the small caravan pulled out and began its journey west. Descending from the high Syrian plateau, they crossed a region the Jews called Galilee. It was lush and green and hugged the great lake of Tiberius. But they were eager to move on, and after a night at the city of Sepphoris, they continued west. Traveling south, they soon broke through mountains and learned that Caesarea would be no more than two hours ahead of them. The travel was slow. Gaius was in the lead wagon with Livia, their pace set by the mules that pulled them. Appius rode out front with two of his guards, viewing the territory with new eyes. This would be his new home. This would be a place—he barely understood—that he would never forget. Soon they saw the aqueduct that fed Caesarea from northern mountains, and they simply followed it south until they saw the city of its destination.

Figure 4.1. Remains of the aqueduct at Caesarea Maritima

Tullus had never seen Caesarea. Of course, stories about it were told throughout Gallica because many had come in order to meet ships from the west bringing supplies and troops into the province. As the wagons entered the city's gates, Tullus felt as if he were entering a world he had barely imagined. The city's

CAESAREA MARITIMA

When the province of Judea was conquered by Rome in 63 B.C. and formed into an administrative district, the Romans permitted the Jews to have remarkable freedom to rule themselves. Such imperial provinces enjoyed the personal attention of the emperor, who then let local leadership rule so long as no rebellion erupted. If conflicts arose, he could deliver a legion to the province to end it. This happened in Judea in A.D. 66.

Judea's first king was Herod the Great, who ruled from 37 B.C. to 4 B.C. One of his aims was to convert Judea into one of Rome's finest provinces. He launched an expensive and massive building program that included not only Roman provincial cities but a complete rebuilding of Jerusalem and its temple.

On the Mediterranean coast he built a deep-water port at a location that had once been a navigation point called Strato's Tower. The harbor was larger than even that at Athens. This permitted Herod to receive large ships from the west, enjoy the immediate support of the Roman army and begin trading with other provinces nearby. Newly developed hydraulic cement, which could set underwater, made the port possible, since it was built directly into the sea. Writers such as Josephus remarked on the beauty of the port and its ambition to inspire visitors who might think of Judea as a primitive frontier province. When ships entered the harbor, they first saw an enormous temple to Augustus built on a hill above it.

The city itself was impressive. Excavations have uncovered warehouses, the foundation of the Augustus Temple, large sections of the quay (or pier), the theater (seating 3,500) and a hippodrome, or horseracing track. The city was large, and today only a small portion has been uncovered. But from what we have seen—such as enormous public architecture, the remains of the pier underwater—we know that in the first century it was a prosperous and important province town.

Figure 4.2. The hippodrome at Caesarea Maritima

original patron, Herod, had built it out of white stone, and it glimmered in the sunlight. The markets were filled with merchants from throughout the Mediterranean. He saw styles of dress and overheard languages he did not recognize. They rode past temples, splendid in their construction, and enormous administrative buildings bustling with Roman clerical workers. Soon he saw what the Romans called *Mare Nostrum*, or "our sea." The city encircled its harbor with a quay and entrance that was nothing short of spectacular. This day three ships rested at anchor. Two were warships, one a freighter hauling goods from some distant place. Tullus understood: this was "their sea," the Roman sea, that no other could claim.

Tullus realized that the Romans in this city were different. They were not soldiers, as he was accustomed to, but men of education, men of influence. They were well dressed in expensive clothes that made Tullus feel as if he were—he didn't know how else to express it—backward. This was a city that managed power and wealth. A city connected to Rome.

He felt himself shrinking as they rode deeper and deeper into the city. He was not like these people. These were the men who told legions like Gallica what they were to do.

The barracks of the legionary outpost was near the port. And while Appius dismounted and entered the main building, Gaius, Livia and Tullus stood near the wagons looking out to sea. The city was also called Caesarea Maritima, with good reason: *Caesarea on the Sea*. A carefully built quay arched into the sea and curved north, making this a deep-water harbor that could welcome the finest Roman vessels. And it was beautiful. Finely dressed Romans and legionary soldiers were standing on its polished granite stone beneath tapestry awnings that shielded them from the heat of the desert sun. The freighter was being unloaded, and large cargoes were hauled along the quay in wagons. As ships entered the port, their first sight was the Temple of Augustus. On a hill facing the harbor, its white marble columns housed the great emperor Augustus's statue. Twice the size of any man, he was clothed in full battle armor, standing in a chariot pulled by two wild horses. There was no mistaking. This was a *Roman* harbor dedicated to the one man whose work built the empire that now ruled the world.

Appius, emerging from the building, returned to the wagons with directions. There was a wooden fort, barely used, that was well protected and guarded, just outside the city. Gaius and the guards would lead the wagons to the small post and unload temporarily while it was determined where they would remain. There were accommodations enough for each of them. Appius was given a room in the barracks and was invited to bring with him an assistant who would make his quarters with the infantry living around the courtyard.

He chose Tullus.

For many days Tullus accompanied Appius as he attended meetings with provincial officials. It was vital, they argued, that incoming Romans understand difficulties that were native to the province. It was called Judea because its largest tribal population called themselves Jews. The Jews cared little for Caesarea—this city had been built only to serve Rome's purposes—but they could be explosively protective of Jerusalem, their sacred city. Uprisings were not uncommon. And to watch things carefully, Rome had refurbished an old fortress that overlooked the Jewish temple in Jerusalem. Troops regularly rotated in and out of the city, watching for any sign of dissent or disturbance.

None of this was news to Appius. Jews lived throughout Syria. Raphana had its own Jewish community, which had a house of gathering for its weekly meetings. Jews were one of the largest minorities even in Rome.

But here, his advisers warned, small tensions could easily become inflamed and burn out of control. This was an explosive province on the fringe of the empire. And while thousands of legionnaires had effectively quieted Syria, Judea had more freedom than it deserved. One day, they said, an inevitable war would arise, and then the empire would need to remove that freedom.

There were idle days, too, when Tullus and Appius had little to do. Appius was a soldier waiting for an assignment that had not yet been invented. Gallica had sent many soldiers in service

JUDEA

Judea was an imperial province that enjoyed its own local rule under Rome until Herod the Great's sons failed to carry on their father's legacy of good (though severe) management and fealty to the empire. Two sons successfully ruled the north of the country (Herod Antipas, Herod Philip), but another named Archelaus failed miserably in the south. In A.D. 6 the Romans removed him and installed Roman governors.

This meant that during the lifetime of Jesus, Tiberius was Rome's emperor; Herod's son Antipas was ruling western Galilee, which Jesus called home; and a Roman governor ruled the center of the country, which included Jerusalem. The governor likely remained in Caesarea for much of the time. But occasionally he traveled to Jerusalem to see the Jewish leadership. There he may have stayed either at Herod the Great's old palace (on the city's west side, just south of the modern Jaffa Gate) or in the Antonia Fortress, built on the temple court's northwest corner (remains can be found on the modern Via Dolorosa in the Sisters of Zion Convent).

Judea was compliant under Rome's rule until A.D. 66, when conflict began and then escalated into a devastating war. Four years later (A.D. 70), Jerusalem was sacked and burned by Roman legions.

to the province, and they had worked with honor. Appius was hopeful that his work would materialize soon and that it would be important.

Caesarea had many distractions. There were athletic games

and gladiatorial contests that were the finest at this far east end of the empire. There was a huge theater, where audiences enjoyed the greatest dramas of the empire. Seated in sculpted seats beneath expansive awnings facing the ocean, they were entertained by singers and actors. Just to the south there was a new horse-racing track, where chariots and skilled horsemen competed for money before cheering crowds. There were markets where anything, indeed *anything*, could be bought, from Ethiopian slaves to Spanish jewelry to spices from India. Each day, as he took in more of the city, Tullus felt as if his eyes could barely absorb another spectacle.

Appius seemed to enjoy showing Tullus the delights of the Roman way, the *Via Romana*, he called it. It was a life carefully built around values of honor, strength and discipline. For Tullus it seemed beautiful, so organized, so intentional, so dramatically different from the rural town of his childhood. He had thought he knew the Romans in Emesa. He now learned he did not. He had thought he knew them in Raphana. This was only a shadow of the real thing he now witnessed in Caesarea. No wonder the Romans ruled the world.

One afternoon Appius approached Tullus with an exuberance that Tullus had not seen before. Tullus was intrigued. Appius, he thought, was coming back to life.

"An arena has been built outside the walls. And we are going."

"An arena? For what purpose? We already have arenas for games, for theater and for horses."

"This is something you have not seen. Nor have I seen it for years. Gladiators have come by sea. They are from Carthage and have recently arrived from Alexandria. Everyone says that they are without parallel anywhere in the empire."

Before he knew it, Tullus was swept up by crowds making their way to the outskirts of Caesarea. And there he saw it. An arena with a tented wall filling with hundreds—no, thousands—of excited spectators. Appius paid a considerable sum for both of them so they might have the best seats, overlooking the center of the oval ring. Roman dignitaries, both men and women, were seated around them, and Tullus thought he caught his first glimpse of the provincial governor. It was all noise and crowds and hawkers selling food and mementos from the day. Tullus saw small boys running about with short wooden swords, copies of the favorite weapon of gladiators.

Suddenly drummers, seated at the end of the arena, silenced the crowd with an ominous, pulsating beat. Horn blowers sounded an alarm that everyone must move behind a strongly built fence that separated the arena from the crowds. Men with swords were stationed every fifty feet.

Two men stepped from a gate tucked between the arena seating. They were enormous men. And while they wore no uniform, they carried weapons Tullus had seen in the legion: short-swords and knives, and small, round shields. They met the cheering crowds with waves and threw their shields to the ground as if they were an encumbrance. The drums began beating again. The crowd went silent, and quickly six slaves ran into the arena, armed only with knives. The gladiators faced them as the slaves spread out and began to circle them. But the gladiators would not be entrapped. They attacked and quickly cut them down. Tullus had not seen blood sport before, and it made him want to retch as six men fell in an instant to the expert skill of these two fighters. A wagon pulled by horses rushed across the sand, and the bodies were heaved into it in a pile. As the wagon pulled away, Tullus saw a heavy stream of blood flowing from its bed.

The crowd was on its feet, cheering. The gladiators raised their blood-stained gladius swords into the air in response. And

BLOOD SPORT

Gladiator games emerged in the Hellenistic period between 150 and 250 years before Christ. Initially they were simple "spectacles" provided by a ruler to thank a city for its support or solicit its interest for future times. Captured slaves or animals usually provided the source of entertainment as skilled men re-created combat with them to show Roman prowess. On occasion the spectacle was a re-creation of some battle where Roman victory could be celebrated.

But soon they evolved into something more complex. The gladiator became a professional fighter, skilled in "blood sport," who could make an enormous name for himself and become quite rich. Gladiator spectacles were very expensive, since the cost of the fighters themselves was high, as were the costs of the victims of the fight: slaves, animals and so forth.

Figure 4.3. Two female gladiators, Amazon and Achilia

It was rare to see women in the arena, but we know it took place. In a famous passage from Suetonius, the historian describes one emperor and his spectacles: "Domitian presented many extravagant entertainments in the coliseum and the circus. Besides the usual two-horse chariot races he staged a couple of battles, one for infantry, the other for cavalry; a sea-fight in the amphitheater; wild-beast hunts; gladiatorial shows by torchlight in which women as well as men took part."[a]

[a]See the Perseus Project for the text of C. Suetonius Tranquillus, "The Lives of the Twelve Caesars," Domitian 4:1 (perseus.tufts.edu).

then the drums began again. Now entered two barbarian slaves, armored and obviously skilled. Tullus thought they were Parthians—he wished they were, but he couldn't be sure. They showed little fear and moved confidently toward the gladiators, who now quickly collected their shields. This would be a real fight, and the crowd knew it. At once the men were engaged in combat, and the outcome seemed uncertain. Tullus could barely make out who was winning amid all the dust and confusion while the crowds were screaming all around him. And then the crowd gasped—Tullus quickly looked back to the arena—one of the barbarians had been impaled by a gladiator and was falling backward. The gladiator shoved him off and then turned on the other slave, whom he dispatched with a single slash. And it was over. Again the Romans had been victorious.

Scene after scene unfolded as Tullus watched. In one instance, a gladiator met a bear single-handed. The bear would not fall after being stabbed. Its claws cut through the air fruitlessly when at last the gladiator's weapon met its mark and the animal crumpled into the sand. Each successive spectacle was more intense than the next. Five Scythian horsemen entered the arena and proudly rode before the crowd, waving their long-swords. They were known for their fine horses and cavalry combat. They knew no gladiator could stand against them. Two men entered the arena and stood ready to face the Scythians, who laughed and rode around them in circles, taunting them, promising to deliver a quick kill. But as they made their charge, archers stepped from the margin, and before the horsemen could attack, arrows flew at their horses and their riders. Horses and horsemen fell in a heap, and the gladiators finished off any who were alive. It was another Roman victory.

Tullus had to look away. *Is this Rome? Do I barely know Appius and the world he came from?*

The bodies were piled on wagons, but by now the arena was thoroughly bloodstained. The drummers began a slow, rhythmic beat that alerted the audience that the final, climatic event was to come. Everyone watched in silence. What surprise was now in store? What new game could be left?

A gate opened. An official waved his hands upward to silence any murmuring. He was announcing two new gladiators, never seen in this part of the world before. Their names were Amazon and Maxilla. The audience gasped. Two women stepped into the arena. Their long hair flowed over their shoulders, and they marched provocatively before the crowds. They wore the combat gear of men and short tunics. In one hand they each carried a brass helmet, in the other a gladius and a circular shield. Tullus was transfixed. *Women in an arena? Women fighting in blood sport? Women dressed like men?*

The crowd stood in silence as a gate swung open. Dwarves! Four dwarves with light armor and knives. Tullus could hear the crowd laughing: *Classic! What could be better?! I can't believe we're so lucky.*

Amazon and Maxilla strapped on their helmets, their hair springing from under the rims and down their backs. They hoisted their round shields onto their left wrists and lowered their short-swords with their right hands. The dwarves approached cautiously. One threw his knife, which bounced off Amazon's shield. And then the whole group of them began to run. The women pursued. Tullus could not watch. But from the laughing and cheering of the crowd he could tell that the deed was done.

But then more drumming. *What's this? More?* Another gate swung open, and this time it was a panther. Black and quick, it had been tormented and starved into an angry killer. Entering the ring, it immediately smelled blood in the sand. It saw the feast of dwarves but then quickly spied the two women moving carefully nearby. They were foe. And the beast knew it.

The panther ran around them in a wide circle, looking for its best opportunity, while the women moved back to back, watching its every move. The panther was crazed and making horrid sounds, to the delight of the audience. The perimeter guards looked nervous and held their shields and swords carefully. This was an unpredictable scene, and anything could happen. The panther might even turn and jump the fence and attack the crowd. Its tail whipped from side to side as it stalked the women. Its eyes never seemed to move. It had one target.

Tullus was transfixed and could not look away. Secretly he prayed that the panther would win, that Roman blood would be spilled this day, that somehow this sport would end unexpectedly. As the panther circled, it closed, tightening its pattern around the women, who turned slowly, watching its eyes. The drummers began a slow, rhythmic beat while the women and the beast studied each other's gestures.

Suddenly the panther sprang without warning. Explosively. And its front paws hit Maxilla's shield directly. The woman flew to the ground on her back, and the beast clearly realized its advantage. Maxilla tried to hide under her shield while the panther was swiping at it, clawing to remove it and gain the target of her neck. The arena grew silent. Amazon flung herself onto the back of the animal and began stabbing at it desperately. In one turn, the panther swiped at her, cutting her arm deeply and throwing her into the sand. But she returned with greater ferocity. The two women and the cat were covered with dirt and blood. Amazon's sword was swinging in the air. Maxilla's screams could be heard by all in the stands. Tullus found it impossible to look away and held his breath.

Then all action stopped.

The crowd was speechless. Tullus did not blink. There were slow, careful movements in the heap of dirty, bloodied flesh. Amazon arose and looked down at the gnarled mess at her feet. Then Maxilla kicked the carcass of the dead beast from her body and stood on her feet. She was soaked in the cat's blood. Pulling off her helmet, she raised her sword to the deafening cheers of a thousand Roman voices.

Tullus had never seen Appius so exultant. He was energized. He had come back to life. Blood sport had revived the spirit of the legionnaire. To be a centurion. To be a Roman. No one wanted to leave; they wanted the moment to continue forever. Together Tullus and Appius followed the crowds back into the city, sharing an exuberance Appius had only felt at the close of a battle. He asked Tullus again and again about his favorite spectacle. He wanted to relive every moment.

"And when the panther had the woman down in the sand—my god, I couldn't believe it. One snap of his jaw and she would have been gone. And then what?" Appius was animated, excited, reveling in the risks taken so near where he had been standing. "It would have been the cat and the other woman alone. Just the two of them. And then what?"

"What then? I think the panther would have bested both of them," Tullus offered.

"I think so too. Perhaps the arena is no place for a woman. But still, it was a sight I shall not soon forget."

As they moved across the city, the crowd dispersed. But Appius had another idea. He wanted to end the day perfectly. To continue to show his young scribe how the *Via Romana* was truly lived. Near the theater he found a street studded with mosaics and sculptures that made clear he had found what he sought: the brothel district of Caesarea.

Figure 4.4. Remains of a single-room shop, or taberna, at Caesarea Maritima

Appius looked at Tullus in an invitation to join him. "I have money. And it will be a day's perfect end."

"But are you sure of this? We could just as easily return to the barracks."

"And miss this? Some of the men told me to find a woman named Venus, who owns a guest house in this district. And that is what we shall do."

Tullus saw the place first. Exotic and graphic sculptures clung to the wall above the door. Together they walked through an opening that led to an enclosed garden and fountain. Frescoes adorned every wall, mostly of nude men and women in scenes Tullus had never imagined. Soon a beautiful woman approached with two chalices of wine and invited them to sit on the fountain pool's enclosure in the cool of the shade. She was enchanting. The wine was refreshing. And the scene was exotic, something Tullus had never imagined for himself. This must be Venus, he thought, the owner and overseer of the guest house. She was mature, elegant, self-assured.

Once they were settled, Venus disappeared quietly, and soon two new women joined them. One chatted gaily with Appius. Within minutes he was following her to the far side of the courtyard, where they disappeared behind a curtain. The other was young, about Tullus's age, and she sat on the fountain wall next to him.

"So you are a stranger to this city?" The woman looked at him

PUBLIC SEXUALITY

Brothels like the one Appius visits with Tullus were common throughout the Roman Empire. They were a part of the "public sexuality" well known in both Greek and Roman culture. Temple participation involving sexual activity, public festivals displaying overt fertility cult items (such as the Bacchus Feasts), and dinner parties for men followed by sexual gameplay with hired women were not uncommon. Erotic poetry, public erotic art, even pottery with erotic images were regular features of Roman life. The Romans felt few scruples about placing limits on male sexuality. Some poets extolled the values of male "explorations" in guesthouses for the sake of healthier families. However, women who belonged to a household were not free to do the same.

Brothels (or buildings devoted to prostitution) were common in virtually every city. They have been excavated in the Holy Land (Bet Sean, or Scythopolis, in southern Galilee provides good examples). But the best examples are without doubt preserved in Pompeii. There brothels have been found nearly intact: exterior advertising sculptures, detailed erotic frescoes and even back rooms complete with private beds.

directly. She was clearly in charge but discreetly so. Her confidence was inviting, not intimidating. Tullus felt his pulse quicken.

"I am. We arrived just weeks ago."

"From the west, I suspect? You look like a man who has traveled greatly. Your accent sounds Greek. Refined. Noble. Not like the men who usually visit us." Tullus saw her look him over and noticed that she appeared to like what she saw.

Figure 4.5. Carved stone bed in a Pompeii brothel

Tullus blushed, not recognizing it as the practiced flattery that it was. He found himself intrigued, drawn, excited. The woman moved closer and poured more wine into his chalice from a pitcher that was cooling in the water of the fountain. She dipped her finger into his chalice, deep into the wine, drew it to her mouth slowly and laughed. She never broke her gaze. Tullus thought she smelled of flowers and liked it. Her long hair was carefully groomed, and he found himself entranced by every detail of her face. She was sitting close. Too close, he thought.

"And what is the best thing you've done this day?" She smiled and rested her slight hand on Tullus's arm. Her fingers were light in their touch, and she drew patterns on his skin. She crossed her legs, and one of her feet slipped behind his calf, beneath the fringe of his tunic.

Tullus was nervous.

"We have just come from the arena. The new one. The spectacle that has arrived from Alexandria." He began speaking rapidly—he knew this—and in a minute he was describing the arena, the horror of it, the dwarves and the panther, and the more he talked the surer he was that whatever had been building between them was beginning to slip away.

She withdrew her hand and folded it into the other that rested on her lap.

Tullus drank again from his chalice and tried to regain his composure. But he knew he did not want to go further with this woman and enact the scenes on the villa walls. It was not because he was afraid of what they might do together. This was all the men of Gallica talked about. They came to guesthouses like this regularly in Raphana. Tullus had never joined them, though he knew he was ready.

It was not what they might do together that worried him. It was what she might see when they were together. And this is what kept him from these houses.

It was Tullus's deepest secret. And he had kept it ever since he left Emesa. There was something about him that no Roman would like, something most Romans scorned. No one in Appius's household knew. And he could barely show it to a woman. Especially a woman like this. A woman who might laugh at him. Who might think him unmanly. It was a reminder to him that he wasn't fully Roman. And never would be.

He was marked.

Tullus was circumcised.

CIRCUMCISION

When Romans thought about the Jewish minority that lived throughout the empire, two things came to mind: their commitment to observing the Sabbath and their tradition of circumcising their sons. Circumcision is the surgical removal a sheath of skin (the foreskin) found at the end of the penis. This was done on the child's eighth day after birth (and is still done today among Jews, Muslims and many Christians).

Circumcision was considered the "tribal mark" of God among the Jews. After Abraham was called into a covenant relationship with God (Gen 12–15) he was circumcised (Gen 17). Genesis 17:10-14 makes the rule explicit: "This is my covenant, which you shall keep, between me and you and your offspring after you: Every male among you shall be circumcised. You shall be circumcised in the flesh of your foreskins, and it shall be a sign of the covenant between me and you. He who is eight days old among you shall be circumcised. Every male throughout your generations, whether born in your house or bought with your money from any foreigner who is not of your offspring, both he who is born in your house and he who is bought with your money, shall surely be circumcised. So shall my covenant be in your flesh an everlasting covenant. Any uncircumcised male who is not circumcised in the flesh of his foreskin shall be cut off from his people; he has broken my covenant" (ESV).

There is no such thing as female circumcision. The term has been wrongly used of the practice among some primitive Islamic groups and African tribes for the surgical removal of the clitoris before a girl reaches puberty (to destroy sexual desire). But this was not a biblical practice, and Jews and Christians abhor it as cruel and disfiguring. This practice is formally called a *clitoridectomy.*

5

Caesarea

Livia noticed the change as well. Appius was coming back to life. He often circulated back to the fort outside town to see that all was well. And yet, oddly, it had not become his home. Nor was Livia still his companion the way she had once been. Appius had emerged from his illness a different man. His wounds had hardened him, or perhaps they had invited something deep in Appius's soul to come to the surface and claim a central place. Appius was businesslike. He had always been efficient, which was why Gaius was such an excellent match for him. But now he expressed even less emotion. Livia thought of it as detachment. He would sit at home and talk for hours about horses. But he would not notice that she was even in the room. Every attempt to draw his attention failed.

Livia was happy for him but also troubled. He rarely looked at her the way he used to. They never embraced. And they rarely talked about things that mattered. His arm still gave him debilitating pain and severely limited his range of motion. But he would not discuss it. In Livia's mind the arrow was still there, threatening Appius's life. Threatening both of their lives. And she wondered whether the wound had made Appius think of himself as incapable in ways in which he was capable before. Perhaps she reminded him of another Appius, another time, another man who had died at Dura. At the very least she knew the arrow had embedded itself in their relationship.

Livia spent most of her days talking to Gaius, which had never been an easy task. Now it was even more difficult. Even Gaius had become sullen and was drawing into himself.

Tullus came to the fort to visit the household more frequently than Appius. His face lit up when he saw each of them. He even had begun to like Gaius and found himself thinking about the slave's strict habits as endearing. Gaius, for instance, hated seeing blood on the floor of his kitchen ("Animals must be cleaned in the market or the garden!"), and to Tullus and Livia this was asking a great deal of the slaves who prepared their food. Blood was always on the floor of a normal kitchen.

Gaius also hated the new clothes that Tullus and Livia had found in Caesarea. To him, the tunics had become too short, too sheer, too glamorous and too expensive. Livia, in his estimation, wore too much makeup.

And why, he thought, did she have to wear a dozen or more bracelets on one arm? Gaius had opinions about everything. And even when he didn't say anything, his eyes told all. He believed Livia was immodest. And he thought Tullus was impulsive and immature. In his mind both failed to understand that how one disciplines one's appetites now determines how one will succeed in life later. "Master your soul, young Tullus, and your arm will take care of itself." These words could have been emblazoned on a wall, they were said so often.

"Is that a new hat?" Tullus had brought home the newest fashion: a stiff-brimmed hat that reminded him of the sun god, Helios. "Are modest head coverings no longer in fashion?" Often Tullus would intentionally bring these things just to provoke

COSMETICS FOR WOMEN

Literary descriptions, burial portraits, frescoes and artifacts from excavations all prove that Roman women wore a great deal of makeup. This included whitening foundations, rouge, mascara, eye shadow (similar to modern *kohl*, from lead sulfide), deodorants, enhanced eyebrows (which in some cases

Figure 5.1. Cosmetic bottles

Figure 5.2. A double cosmetic bottle

almost met above the nose), teeth whiteners and perfumes. Historians suspect that women did not color their lips. Some men viewed the overuse of cosmetics as implying that a woman was immoral and so preferred their wives not use them. However, their use was widespread, particularly among women in the upper classes.

Gaius. And Livia often stood by just to see Gaius rise to the moment. Livia didn't think all his reactions were genuine. Gaius did have opinions, but when he expressed them in exaggerated forms it had become a game. One day she appeared at dinner with well over thirty bracelets on her right arm. It was so tedious that she couldn't eat with them, and she complained to Gaius how fashion took such a toll. They batted back and forth the "right" number of bracelets a woman should wear for at least fifteen minutes.

Livia swore she caught a smile pass over the old slave's face.

In Appius's absence, Livia and Tullus had found a deepening friendship. It began as they discussed Appius and his changes, but it shifted as he made fewer and fewer appearances in the household. He was busy with the affairs of the province and so seemed less involved with the affairs of his familia. Tullus would spend the day with Appius. And when Appius went out with other centurions working in the province, often Tullus wandered back to the fort just to see Livia.

"I am not sure if Appius even knows why we are here anymore." She was standing in the courtyard, helping Tullus unload provisions he had purchased in the markets. "I haven't seen him in days, and when he is here, he's not really here."

"He has returned to life, Livia. He has regained so much that he lost. It's the responsibility he holds again—and the confidence of the tribunes who assist the governor. He was a man who almost died. And it was by his strength that he recovered. And he is recovering still. Believe me."

"But we see none of it."

"We will. And in the meantime, we simply need to maintain his household as we always have. You, Gaius and me. We need to live as if he were present, obedient to his wishes even though he is not here to express them. This is how we honor him."

THE HELIOS HAT AND FASHION

Every generation signals its differences from the previous generation with innovations in clothing, hairstyle and even music choices. These changes today are very rapid—more rapid, perhaps, than at any time in history. Fashions change within a couple of years or a season, and we think little of it. A hairstyle popular fifteen years ago would rarely be worn today by people who care about such things.

The Hellenistic era introduced a number of changes to traditional clothing. Romans enjoyed long, sweeping clothing that wrapped fluidly around the body. This replaced draped garments that hung down directly from the shoulders to the feet in one robe-like piece. Short togas with high-laced sandals were popular choices in the first century. And we know that stiff-brimmed hats were just making their appearance. The stiff brim reminded many of a halo, a symbol that evoked the sun god, Helios.

Because the hat symbolized assimilation into Hellenistic culture and could refer to a Greek god, many Jewish leaders opposed it (see 2 Maccabees 4:7-17) and compared its use with a profound loss of Jewish faith. Such men (so argues 2 Maccabees) also neglected the temple sacrifices and worship and instead were infatuated with the gymnasium and events such as the "call to the discus." Such things were labeled an extreme form of Hellenization and completely "unlawful."

"And in the meantime? I am to wait without hope?"

"There is always hope." Tullus turned toward her, moved closer and took her hands. "There is always hope, Livia. Appius is committed to us, and now he shows it by giving us money to pay for what we need. We are still a part of his familia—he has not sent us off to find a new life without us. He has not discharged any of us. He has not abandoned us."

"But hope begins to thin when there is little promise. When he left on marches with the legion, I always knew he was eager to come back to me. He always promised me as I kissed him at our gate. It was a kiss of longing, of incompletion, that promised something more would come. I have lost that promise. I know he rarely thinks about me, rarely wonders where I am. Rarely imagines himself with me."

"You are not alone, Livia. You will never be alone."

"I do have Gaius and you." She paused. "But especially you. You have always been faithful to me, Tullus. Always kind, always honorable. Not like the men who look at me on the street. *You know me.*"

Tullus felt something new. He was looking directly at Livia, and a distance had closed. An invisible wall was being dismantled, one built by both of them, but him in particular. He considered ignoring the wall entirely, moving deeper into this new and forbidden territory.

Tullus looked at her with different eyes. He noticed the scented oil she wore, making her skin shine radiantly in the sun and emitting the faint aroma of jasmine. Her eyes, moist and amber, looked at him in a way that anticipated something more, something he was not sure how to express. Time seemed suspended. He was afraid and thrilled, and wanted to yield to the pull. Where it would lead, he did not know. Nor was he sure he cared.

That last thought flooded him with adrenaline and fear. He stepped back.

THE ROMAN *FAMILIA*

The Roman *familia* was an economic or social unit whose protection and preservation was the highest order of commitment for Rome. It was not limited to the intimate arrangements we know as the "nuclear family" today. A better translation might be a "household," which included spouses, children and various types of slaves. In some cases this could consist of unrelated people whose cooperation made them "one." Therefore when Appius refers to Tullus as belonging to his familia, he is making a statement that has less to do with emotion than with commitment (although emotional attachment often played an important role).

Figure 5.3. Painting of a woman

The *paterfamilias* was the head of the household (hence the "father" of the familia). Roman society was strongly patriarchal, and the male head of the family could exercise enormous power. He could discharge or divorce his wife easily; he accepted or rejected the children born in his household; he could even "expose" (or kill by exposure) any newborn child he did not want. He had complete authority over his slaves and could sell, punish or even kill them, since laws respecting persons did not apply to them. Appius was the paterfamilias of his familia.

And just then he saw Gaius. Impatient because he wanted what Tullus carried—but also wearing a knowing scowl, awareness and alarm in his eyes as he glanced back and forth, sizing up each of them. Gaius knew. Nothing escaped him. He knew. And he didn't like what he saw.

Livia turned quickly when she saw Tullus turn toward the door. She also saw Gaius, blushed, and with her eyes down walked quickly past him and into their rooms. Gaius followed her.

This moment shifted the equilibrium of the entire household. Tullus felt sure the rest of the slaves knew. Gaius seemed alert and awakened from his darkness. There was a new reality in the house, one as dangerous as any Parthian. If the arrow of Dura had nearly killed Appius, Gaius thought, this new arrow—shot perhaps by Eros himself—could lead to something equally violent. For Livia, for Gaius and most certainly for Tullus.

Tullus was chastened. And his visits became less frequent, shorter and more intentional. He once sent a courier from the main barracks to give Gaius the weekly money he needed. He carried no word to be delivered to Livia.

"But certainly Tullus said something. Surely he mentioned me as he sent you out."

"No, he did not. He told me to be quick and to return at once. Not to linger *with anyone.*" Which Livia interpreted to mean her and her alone. Gaius turned his attention to the courier, and they negotiated their business. Gaius was holding a note from Tullus that the courier had read aloud. But Livia began to worry. What if Tullus was in trouble?

The courier left their rooms, Gaius walking with him. Livia picked up the small papyrus scrap Tullus had penned and ran her fingers over its expert letters. She could not read, but she knew that these marks could re-create the voice of their author. On a corner the ink had smudged and captured the fingerprint

PAPYRUS AND WAX

Writing instruments had developed significantly in the first century. Students would commonly own a wooden tablet with a thick wax coating on one side. This was used with a wooden stylus that etched the surface of the wax for temporary writing that could be later removed.

For documents the preferred writing surfaces were papyrus and vellum. Papyrus is a reed-like plant that was harvested along the Nile delta in Egypt. The inner pith was split, soaked in water and then laid out in two layers set at right angles to each other to make flat sheets, then sanded and dried. It made a remarkably durable and smooth paper that could be cut to fit commercial sizes. Vellum was sheepskin that was scraped, cured, stretched and dried. This was far more expensive and was used for permanent documents.

Figure 5.4. Wall painting from Pompeii showing a couple with writing implements, she with a stylus and wax tablet and he with a scroll

of its writer. Livia pressed it with her own hand, slipped her finger where his had once been and held it close to her face. And then she decided. She would follow the courier back through town just to confirm that Tullus was safe. Nothing more. She just wanted to see whether Tullus was well.

The courier was in no hurry. No one knew the duration of his journey or the length of his stay at the fort, so he wandered leisurely for a time through the center of Caesarea. Livia kept a distance but never lost sight of him. His unhurried pace meant her movements were not obvious and she could pause at merchant stalls lining the narrow city streets.

Eventually the courier began to walk decisively toward the city port. Livia knew his destination had to be the barracks of the centurions, where Appius and Tullus worked. But danger loomed. What if Appius met her unexpectedly? How would she explain being at the military camp unaccompanied, a young single woman, officially attached to Appius but not looking for him? Common infantry might find her and think wrongly of her. In her impulsive haste she had failed to even veil herself and was clothed only in a common household tunic and sandals. Nothing that an honorable woman would wear in public.

The courier entered through the main gateway leading to the provincial offices. Livia watched him from the corner of a nearby building and knew she could not go further. Guards stood outside the gate. Not only would they forbid her passage, but they also might detain her and inquire after her intentions. But she did not turn back. She waited in hiding until she could no longer discipline her own impulses. Then she stepped out and headed toward the gate.

When the governor had summoned Appius for a meeting that morning, Appius quickly called Tullus to his side and made sure that each of them were ready for a formal meeting. Tullus brought a wax tablet and stylus for quick note taking. He wore his best tunic and with it attached the military belt that had been given to him at Gallica. It was handsomely tooled with the insignia of the legion and held a sheath in which Tullus wore a knife. When he arrived at Appius's quarters, he saw him struggling with his uniform. Swiftly and without comment, Tullus attended to the parts that Appius could not reach. Together they looked orderly, fit and prepared.

"When we enter the governor's villa, his personal guard will escort us to his reception rooms. You shall not speak unless asked to do so. Read nothing aloud unless I request it." Appius seemed nervous and yet confident. He rarely saw the governor, in part because the governor was aloof and rarely went about with the troops he commanded.

"And do I address him when we meet?"

"Do not. I will speak for us. You are but my shadow."

"And if I see something in writing that you need to know before you make any agreements?"

"Then speak out. Never turn your back toward him, never whisper so that he cannot hear. Ask if it might be of help to read aloud what is before you." Appius relied on Tullus's reading ability more than he would admit. The governor was not trustworthy. He had climbed to this post over many Roman bodies, most of which he had killed. And in this province he was known as calculating and merciless.

"We do not know his purposes this morning. We must be prepared for anything. But we also must be prepared for something he wishes to hide from us."

Together they crossed into the courtyard of the main barracks and moved toward the far north end, where the governor kept his permanent residence. It was an enormous building, long and elegant. The villa was carefully situated within the walls of the barracks and guarded by many legionnaires who were as ambi-

PONTIUS PILATUS

Following the removal of Herod the Great's son Archelaus from central Judea in A.D. 6, governors, or procurators, assigned by Rome ruled the province. These men generally had a military background and were supported by legionary and auxiliary troops assigned to work with them. In Judea they lived in Caesarea Maritima, which was well connected to communication networks and re-created a secure and well-protected "Roman" way of life. When they needed to conduct business with Jewish leaders, they traveled to Jerusalem and either lived in the Antonia Fortress attached to the Temple or used Herod the Great's old palace on the western side of the city.

Figure 5.5. Aerial view of remains of Herod's palace at Caesarea Maritima

Pontius Pilatus (also known as Pontius Pilate) was the fifth governor of Judea and ruled from A.D. 26–36. He was well known to the prominent Jewish historian of the period, Josephus. And his conflicts with Jewish leaders were notorious. When he first came to Judea, he tried to demonstrate his authority by bringing Roman standards (decorated military symbols mounted on a pole and carried by a legionnaire) into the Temple. The Jewish leaders were outraged and saw this as a pagan intrusion into their temple (something that Rome had promised not to do). When Pilate faced off with them in Jerusalem, Jewish leaders knelt before him and declared that they would rather be killed by the sword than see their temple profaned with Roman pagan symbols.

Pilate had met his match and backed down in order to avoid a major diplomatic setback. In the end he learned to work with the Jews, and because he served for ten years while Caiaphas was the high priest, we assume the two men knew how to collaborate in order to keep the province peaceful. Caiaphas reflects the political savvy we see in Pilate. When people saw the popularity of Jesus, some of the leaders complained, "What are we to do? For this man [Jesus] performs many signs. If we let him go on thus, every one will believe in him, and the Romans will come and destroy both our holy place and our nation." Caiaphas said, "You know nothing at all; you do not understand that it is expedient for you that one man should die for the people, and that the whole nation should not perish" (John 11:47-50 RSV).

Jesus was crucified when Pilate was governor of Judea and Caiaphas was high priest in Jerusalem.

tious as this governor. They wanted to follow him to his next assignment and become his permanent guard in a grand city such as Ephesus or Sardis, perhaps even Rome.

Immediately inside the front gate was a courtyard, open to the sky and leading to gardens and fountains. Men were plastering and painting the inner walls, improving on what had been inherited from the previous ruler. Artisans were sketching the outlines of characters that would enliven frescoes yet to be painted. Clearly the governor liked Hercules. One entire wall of the garden was being sketched out to depict a drinking competition between Hercules and Bacchus, the god of wine. In the first frame the mighty Hercules dominated his rival with threatening gestures. In the final frame Hercules was drunk and defeated, his sword fallen, his bravado gone. Bacchus laughed as he held aloft a chalice decorated with grapes.

"His name. What do I say if he *addresses me*?" Tullus had lowered his voice.

"Do not use his name. A slave is never permitted to refer to it. He is your lord. That is enough."

Within minutes a senior tribune approached from an inner chamber. He was immaculately dressed and looked to be the governor's assistant.

"Pontius Pilatus will see you." He turned, seeming to expect that they would follow his pace and direction.

Inside, Pilatus was sitting on a dais that elevated him above his audience. He was a short man who (gossip said) made up for his height by the severity of his rule. When Appius entered, he was introduced as "Appius of Attalia, former primus pilus of Legio Tertia Gallica." Pilatus stood and stepped down to greet them. Tullus was not introduced.

"I hear you are wounded, Appius of Gallica, and your arm is of no use. Is this true?" Tullus was stunned. *These are Pilatus's first words?* The guards attending the meeting looked at the floor. Tullus did the same.

"So the physicians say. I took an arrow in Dura-Europos when my cohort rescued the fort from Parthians."

"But you took it in the back, no? Were you not facing your enemy?"

"He was in hiding, lord."

"And you were uncovered, without armor?"

"I was."

"You were at war, uncovered and unaware that the Parthians were not defeated?"

"Two were in hiding and none of us could see them in—"

"Is this how you train our men? To bare themselves naked before all is secure?"

"No. This was an error. But the gods have spared me." At this the guards looked up, while Pilatus paced in front of his dais. He seemed satisfied.

"Very well. Are you ready to serve me and so serve the emperor?"

"As you wish. I led Legion Gallica and so can lead any you give me."

"So you are willing to do as I wish. I desire for you to command a small town in what the Jews call Galilee. It is small but important. It is from here that we collect many of our taxes in the north. And yet the region is a nest of fighters. You will take thirty of our men. And when you arrive, you will be welcomed by those who manage our tax revenue in that area. They will arrange for your needs." He paused. "Are you encumbered?" It seemed like an afterthought, as if Pilatus were trying to fill in gaps about what he didn't know.

"I have a small familia consisting of a few slaves. There are no attachments."

"Very well. My men will supply you with wagons and horses. And to begin with I will send extra troops to stay until you are secure." Pilatus handed Appius a sealed scroll as he continued to discuss the particulars of the move. Appius slipped the scroll to Tullus, who quietly broke the seal and unrolled it, skimming its details. Appius had been demoted—the words were clear—and this would affect his pay. But he was free to gain as he might from the taxes, so long as the province was paid its due. The town they were going to was called Capernaum. But the scroll said nothing specific about it except that previous soldiers had found it difficult. There was nothing here that Appius needed to know immediately. Tullus rolled it back up, and Appius looked at him eagerly. Tullus nodded. And then the meeting was over.

Pilatus walked with the two men as they left the villa. The governor began to say how he was eager to see the progress of his gardens and to show Appius the clever theme that would grace his walls. The guards accompanied them as they entered the center courtyard.

But the senior tribune stood apart. He had heard something, an unexpected commotion coming from the main gate. The guards had been yelling, but now seemed to have it under control. So he went on, unobtrusively sending two of his personal guards toward the gate.

Appius saluted the governor and promised that he would bring success to Galilee. Tullus made no gestures, remaining behind the centurion.

"I want you to leave within the week. I want no trouble in this region. And it is a territory that favors making trouble." These were Pilatus's final words.

Appius left the gardens and walked through the small, skylit courtyard. Ahead four soldiers were holding someone who was struggling in their grasp. Tullus moved to Appius's side as they entered the gate. And there they saw Livia: disheveled, roughly held by the guards, with panic in her eyes.

6

From Caesarea to Capernaum

•◇•

Appius interrupted the scene at the gate where the tribune's two guards had clearly taken over. Four armed men were now surrounding Livia, who was between them in the dirt. "Stand at ease. I know this woman." Tullus exercised enormous control not to get involved and tried to look indifferent.

The two regular gate guards immediately stepped away, backing against the stone wall. They looked as if they wanted to disappear. They knew their rank, and they recognized Appius from other events at the barracks. But the two soldiers who had come from the tribune's staff had considerable legionary service. Appius did not know them, but he assumed they would soon be made centurions. They were older, experienced and self-assured.

And they did not back off. One held Livia by the hair as she knelt, clearly in pain, at his feet.

"What is your concern here, centurion?" The soldier holding Livia didn't move. He was firmly planted in the sandy gate-road.

"She belongs to my familia. Stand at ease." It had been months since Tullus had seen Appius like this. This was the primus pilus he knew. This was Appius of Gallica, not Appius of Dura. Appius quickly glanced back into the courtyard. Pilatus and the tribune were watching.

The soldier still did not move, staring at Appius.

Appius stepped closer and now spoke inches from his face. "She is mine. And I have given you an order." Tullus could see the anger rise in his face. He knew this was a moment Appius could not take lightly. "Release her. Now." Tullus could see spit hit the soldier's face as Appius's intensity mounted. Appius had now rested his hand on the hilt of his gladius.

"Release her."

The soldier looked into the courtyard. He glanced down at Livia and then back at Appius, appearing to weigh his options. Tullus thought he must be wondering: *Was this an opportunity to show strength? To show his readiness for promotion? Or would his insubordination cripple his future?*

The second soldier now had stepped out of the way completely and joined the gate guards. He expected blood.

"What is your business with her?" The soldier scowled at Appius. Looking Appius in the eye, he then let his gaze migrate down to Appius's left shoulder. Then, feigning pity, he gave a wry, secretive smile.

"That is of no regard to you." Appius took another step closer and was almost pressing against the man, armor to armor. The next sound was unmistakable: that of Appius drawing his gladius partway out of its sheath. The next seconds would mean everything. One man might soon be dead.

No one seemed to breathe. Everyone waited to see who would back off and whose career would be ruined.

"STAND DOWN!" Appius shouted in the man's face, and with his right hand he grabbed the guard's wrist that was holding Livia's hair. He twisted the wrist backward as he continued to stare at the man. "I will break it if I must." His tone was uncompromising, and his strength was apparent. Appius had decided. He would stand or fall in this gate.

Quietly the senior tribune left Pilatus's side and began walking briskly toward the scene. This conflict had now become unseemly. The standoff would not serve anybody. It had to end. A crowd had formed outside the gate and was ready for the entertainment of two Roman soldiers fighting with a woman between them.

The soldier reached for his sword, but Appius was ahead of him. With his left hand Appius grabbed its hilt and pulled it partway from the guard's belt. When the soldier's tried to reach it, he only felt the sharp edge of his own blade slicing deeply through his palm. He winced, released Livia with his other hand, freed himself from the centurion and stepped back. Blood was flowing freely from his hand. As he let loose a storm of curses at Appius, the tribune stepped between the two men.

Livia scrambled to Tullus and fell at his feet. Tullus looked at her with a confusion of feelings. Should he protect her? Embrace her? Care for her? Be indifferent in front of the province leaders? Could he even kneel down to see if she was hurt? He didn't know his role, and so he stood impassive. But he could see that she was covered with sand. The shoulder of her tunic was torn, and somehow the soldier's blood had splattered it.

"Axius of Carthage, help me understand what I see here." The tribune was not amused.

"We were arresting a peasant slave who tried to enter the barracks against our orders."

"Axius, now help me understand your difficulty with our centurion." The tribune moved to stand alongside Appius, and the two senior men squared off against the soldier, who was now holding his clenched fist as blood oozed between his fingers. He did not otherwise acknowledge the pain or the blood that was now staining his tunic and running down his leg.

COMPETING FOR HONOR

The conflict between Axius and Appius is a shame/honor conflict. The aim of ancient Mediterranean societies was to accumulate honor and avoid shame, and this was pursued at all costs. In this instance, Axius hopes to accrue honor from the conflict because he has an audience of highly honored leaders watching him. If he does well, they will honor him and he will *advance* in society. But it is a risky gamble, since Appius likewise needs to establish his honor as a centurion newly assigned to serve the governor. And a challenge from a subordinate has toxic shame. For Appius to succumb to his threat or to be defeated in any way would mean he would regress or descend through shame. If the challenge had gone much further, Appius would have had to kill the soldier to save himself.

However, Appius makes a brilliant move. Rather than kill the soldier, he shows him mercy by wounding him and so shames him more deeply and gains even greater honor for himself.

Roman societies also believed in limited good and limited honor. Honor was something Appius and Axius were competing for. Only the most delicate resolution could have enabled them to *share* any honor that was available before them at this moment. But both could not come away fully "honored." One would have to incur shame.

This conflict is not about Livia per se. It is not about Appius's affection for her. She is his property, and another man is presuming on it, exploiting it, dishonoring it. Appius is protecting himself, not Livia.

"I did not recognize him."

"But you were in the audience with the governor. You could hear what was said about his role in the province. And can you not recognize a centurion's uniform when it is before you? Just because we are not in a legion here does not mean that rank has no meaning. Are these things not clear in your mind?"

"They are, my lord."

"Go to the physicians. You are fortunate this centurion did not kill you. He offered you mercy, or else you would be lying here at our feet. This has been a poor day for you, Axius of Carthage. Leave us."

The tribune turned to Appius and saw Tullus and Livia nearby. "Go prepare yourself to move. You depart in five days." The tribune seemed to want to be done with the episode. He had stood by Appius, but the scene had tarnished his own reputation in some manner.

Tullus could see that the tribune was confused about why Appius willing to risk so much for a peasant woman. The tribune was left with questions he did not ask, and his face showed it.

Appius nodded to the tribune, and together they watched the defeated soldier walk away from the gate, his shoulders slumped. He knew he would never become a centurion after this, and Appius would never forget his name or face.

Tullus knelt and brought Livia to her feet, looking her over for injuries. She seemed to be paralyzed by the scene. Appius looked at her, then at Tullus, and back again. But then his eyes betrayed a look that Livia read quickly. She pulled herself away from Tullus and began brushing the dirt from her clothes and straightening her hair.

▪ ▪ ▪

For many weeks the provincial leaders had been preparing for the staffing of Capernaum. And when the request from Gallica arrived, they saw Appius's arrival as a perfect solution to their need: they could now provide a centurion to Galilee without depleting their own leadership. None of the centurions in Caesarea wanted to go there. Appius did not have their knowledge. There was no reason to brief him on the attitudes and suspicions of the rest of the troops.

On the day of their departure, two Roman wagons pulled by mules were filled and ready to leave by midday at the fort where Gaius and the household were staying. Tullus was with them. Appius was with the soldiers assigned to him at the barracks in town, and they were to be accompanied by fifteen cavalrymen, who would ride as temporary escorts. Three wagons would carry the soldiers' large tents, tools, food and extra weapons. The permanent men joining Appius were young and very inexperienced. It was likely that some were trying to make their way into one of the legions and so hoped that by serving with Appius they might find a home in Gallica. One man did have legionary experience, Marcus of Sardis, and he was assigned to work as Appius's military assistant and personal guard. Marcus was a lot like Tullus in many ways. He could read, and he had a thoughtful demeanor. But he also resembled Appius himself as a younger man: tough, strong and possessing a quick temper.

Marcus had been at the gate during the conflict with Axius, and the two of them had risen through the ranks together. Marcus confided to Appius that he knew Axius well and knew how violent he was. Promotion to centurion was Axius's life ambition, and now, Marcus believed, that dream was ruined. "The man will remember this, Appius. He does not forget."

All five wagons and the troops met on the main road leading north out of Caesarea. It followed the city's aqueduct for many miles, but then the highway went its own way as it cut a path through a range of mountains. When it entered a wide valley, the road continued north through low hills until it found another valley. When they turned east, they could see in the distance a prominent hill and the city of Sepphoris, the capital of Galilee. There they stopped to refresh themselves and to have Appius meet the Jewish ruler who oversaw this region.

THE VIA MARIS

The route Appius follows is called the Via Maris, or Way of the Sea. This was an ancient highway used for centuries to bring travelers from the high plains of the deserts (near Damascus) down the coast and on to Egypt. Capernaum stood right on this highway and so made an excellent base from which to collect taxes. In the first century the Romans knew the value of this road and rebuilt and reinforced it using the highest standards.

His name was Herod Antipas.

He belonged to one of the legacy families of the Jews—his father reigned at the founding of the province and was responsible for much of the truly impressive building that could be seen. According to Marcus, Antipas was not a congenial ruler. Thirty years earlier his brother had bested him when their father died, and Rome gave the lion's share of the province to his older brother. Antipas had been given western Galilee—a consolation prize.

Sepphoris had all the markings of a town being rebuilt with intentional design, with its fine public buildings and excellent water systems.

Antipas had his own palace there, and Appius marveled at its splendor and the size of its staff. It seemed clear that this man was wealthy and that he used his position to prosper himself.

HEROD ANTIPAS

The Romans built the province of Judea with the help of a wealthy man named Antipater (also called Antipas), who hailed from the southern deserts of Idumea. Antipater was married to the Arab Cypros, and together they had four sons (Phasael, Herod, Joseph and Pheroras) and one daughter (Salome). Antipater's oldest son, Herod (called "the great," as in "eldest"), was proclaimed king of the province by the Roman senate in 40 B.C. but only gained rule over the province with the help of the Roman army in 37 B.C.

Herod the Great had multiple wives and various children, and he suspected three of his sons of treachery. But he intended to make his primary heir Antipas (named after his grandfather), his youngest son, born to a Samaritan named Malthrace. In doing this he completely bypassed Antipas's older brothers Philip and Archaelaus (both born to Cleopatra of Jerusalem). In the spring of 4 B.C. Herod died, but rather than give the kingship to Antipas he changed his will and divided the province among these three sons.

Herod's will was hotly contested in Rome, and many members of the dynasty were lobbying for influence. Herod's sister, Salome, was successful not only in winning over the Emperor Augustus's wife Livia but also in persuading the emperor of Archaelaus's superior loyalty. Grateful for her influence, Augustus awarded her 500,000 pieces of coined silver and the tax revenue of a half-dozen Judean cities. She, of course, was cultivating her own wealth and interest in Judea.

The young Antipas was left as a subordinate ruler of western Galilee, subject to his older half-brother, who was the official representative of the Jews to Rome. (Antipas's other brother Philip ruled eastern Galilee.) Antipas was also given the land abutting the east side of the Jordan River called Perea. But in Rome he had successfully contested his brother's title of "king," and this led to a sharp division between them.

In the Gospel story, this means that his southern region of Perea put Antipas in direct contact with John the Baptist, who criticized Antipas's marriage to Herodias, his brother Philip's wife (see Mk 6:18-29 for details). But rumors also flew about Jesus and John. Jesus had begun his ministry with John the Baptist, and it was John's arrest that led Jesus to leave the Jordan River area and move to Galilee. Antipas knew of a disturbing rumor, which the Gospels record. Apparently, when Antipas heard about the popularity of Jesus, some told him, "John the Baptist has been raised from the dead, and that is why miraculous powers are at work in him [Jesus]" (Mk 6:14).

There was also a Roman barracks in Sepphoris, and the small entourage spent the night there. Appius met the commander, who filled him in on Antipas's ambitions, controllability, and what Appius might expect when he took up residence in Capernaum. The commander confided that he didn't like the Jewish ruler. Neither, apparently, did many of the people he ruled. His most recent controversy was his opposition to a so-called Jewish prophet named John. John had harassed Antipas

SEPPHORIS OF GALILEE

The Via Maris was the main highway that ran through the province of Judea. In Galilee it could be found in the beautiful Bet Netofah Valley, where on a prominent hill stood Sepphoris (Heb. *Zippori*), a city Josephus once called "the ornament of all Galilee." Sepphoris had been ruined in war in 4 B.C. but was rebuilt by Herod Antipas beginning in 3 B.C. and was restored to be Galilee's "ornament." Later Antipas built Tiberius on the Sea of Gali-

Figure 6.1. An aerial view of Sepphoris

lee to be his new capital, but bureaucrats no doubt lived in both cities.

Until the building of Tiberius, Sepphoris was the capital of the region and the likely residence of Herod Antipas. The Gospels do not refer to this city, but because it was under construction throughout Jesus' life, it is common for scholars to suggest that Jesus and his father worked there as builders. Nazareth is only about a ninety-minute walk from Sepphoris.

It is likely that some of the wives of Herod's staff were followers of Jesus and even helped pay his expenses. Luke records the following: "After this, Jesus traveled about from one town and village to another, proclaiming the good news of the kingdom of God. The Twelve were with him, and also some women who had been cured of evil spirits and diseases: Mary (called Magdalene) from whom seven demons had come out; Joanna the wife of Chuza, the manager of Herod's household; Susanna; and many others. These women were helping to support them out of their own means" (Lk 8:1-3). Joanna very likely lived in Sepphoris with her husband, Chuza. Along with Mary from Magdala, Joanna experienced profound healing from Jesus and was grateful.

Today visitors can see the splendor of this ancient city, since excavations have been under way for decades. A tremendous theater seating four thousand, numerous public buildings, colonnaded streets and a large number of residences are signals of Sepphoris's wealth and prestige. It was also fully Jewish, and remnants of Jewish life, seen especially in the number of Jewish ritual baths and ritually pure stoneware, tell us that here fidelity to Jewish religious custom and "modern" ways were forging an alliance.

over Antipas's abandoning his young wife in order to marry his brother's wife. In order to silence John, Antipas had him arrested and killed. But in truth, it seemed that this did not silence him. John had many followers throughout Judea who were agitating for judgment on Antipas. And rumors were widespread that after Antipas killed John, the prophet had returned from the dead to haunt the ruler. What's more, another prophet had arisen, who sounded a lot like John and was now based in Galilee. Antipas was wary of him, too. Jewish prophets, Antipas told Appius, were always to be viewed with suspicion.

The next morning Appius and his party departed from Sepphoris and were soon again climbing through more hills and descending through valleys.

CANA OF GALILEE

For centuries visitors to Galilee have been shown the Arab village of Khirbet Qana and been told that this is the site of the New Testament water-and-wine miracle in John 2. But many have doubted the accuracy of this identification. Recent research has found another site, just north of Sepphoris, that may actually be the correct location. Today archaeologists are working to uncover the remains of this site and to determine its identification.

They passed the village of Cana, which gave them resupply. Then, descending rapidly between dramatic cliffs, they arrived at the great inland sea, the Sea of Tiberius. Its coastline was dotted with fishing villages that would be the immediate concern of Appius as he oversaw the commerce and taxation of the area.

From Tiberius they continued north along the coast, and passing the village of Magdala, they eventually arrived at Capernaum on the lake's north shore. All these and other coastal villages would soon become familiar to them. The scene was

Figure 6.2. The hills of Arbel

beautiful—but also ominous. Everywhere the buildings were made of black stone, debris tossed from a now-extinct volcano.

As they came to the north shore of the Sea of Tiberius, Appius commented a number of times that the black stone troubled him. Was this a portent from the gods, a sign that darkness ruled these lands? Was this why others at Caesarea did not want to come to this place? Had the gods cursed his new home? Soon his enthusiasm for the beauty of Galilee gave way to caution.

Previously, Roman patrols had come to Capernaum from Sepphoris, but they had not stayed long. And now the little village would be absorbing a truly threatening occupation. Forty-five Roman troops along with a centurion were moving into town.

Marcus already had made arrangements through a courier to

MAGDALA

Perhaps the most important Galilee discovery in the past decade has been in Magdala. In 2004 Jerusalem's well-known Pontifical Institute Notre Dame decided it wanted to build a Catholic retreat center in Galilee similar to Notre Dame of Jerusalem. Catholic leaders located four plots of land (twenty acres) in an area north of Tiberius along the Galilee coast that the Jews called Migdal and the Arabs named Al-Majdal, both stemming from the ancient memory of Magdala. They bought the land and began work but had no idea that just a few feet beneath their feet was the first-century town of Magdala, the home of Mary (from) Magdala (see Mt 27:56; Mk 15:40; Lk 8:2, etc.). The village was a

Figure 6.3. Mosaic found at Magdala with image of a boat

commercial fish-trading city. Its name may have come from the Hebrew *migdal*, which means "tower." Fish were preserved by salting and stacking them in towers, and from these stocks shipments could be made to destinations far from the sea.

Magdala is today evolving into a model of how to preserve an ancient site that can serve the needs of scholars and pilgrims. Already archaeologists have discovered a well-preserved first-century synagogue complete with impressive mosaics and rare painted walls. They have also located a menorah relief that may be one of the best in Israel. The village itself has been found complete with markets, baths, villas and a harbor. Moreover, a retreat center for three hundred people and an ecumenical chapel dedicated to the women who followed Jesus are being built in what will be a $100 million project. Already over one thousand volunteers from around the world have dug at Magdala. The website for the excavation is magdalaisrael.wordpress.com/about. The pilgrim website for visitors is magdalacenter.com.

provide a place for Appius and his household while he scouted out an area for the troops to build camp. Meanwhile the fifteen cavalry broke into pairs and rode the perimeter of the town as well as through its main streets in an effort to assess the security of the place. They returned assured that the village had been pacified. Marcus recommended they camp in a dry field just east of the village along the lake. This would give them an excellent water supply and quick access to the main road. There was agreement to this suggestion, and within hours the men were busy constructing a camp plan, a defensive perimeter and latrine ditches.

"And what have you found for us, Marcus?" Appius had surveyed the camp plan, approved it and then found Marcus for directions. The camp was good but would be temporary. There were not enough men to build and defend a fort. They would have to move as soon as they could. His question now to Marcus indicated that his own household was now on his mind.

"There is a small villa on the edge of the village, owned by a Jewish merchant. It's surrounded by a sturdy wall, has a sound courtyard, a neglected garden and about seven rooms on its perimeter. He is willing to rent it to you on favorable terms. He only

Figure 6.4. An aerial view of Capernaum today

asks one thing: that there be no idols brought into the house." At Appius's questioning look, Marcus explained that this was the pejorative term the Jews used for the Roman and Greek gods.

"No idols? Is this the Jewish sensitivity in this province that knows no compromise?"

"It is. And when I remember the number of times Pilatus has offended these people, I wonder whether we shouldn't correct the mistake."

"But that is asking me to abandon who I am. I will not. Tell this man if he wants my money he must let me do what I will with the place. Otherwise I will look elsewhere." Appius had hauled his collection of Apollo statues all the way from Raphana. Many of them even came from his home in Attalia before that.

"This will make your house 'unclean' to the Jews, and they will hesitate to see you there."

"Unclean? I am clean enough. And Gaius makes my house cleaner than I like, to tell the truth."

"This is ritual uncleanness. It has nothing to do with dirt. Some of the Jews believe that when they have contact with certain things, such as dead bodies, certain foods, Gentile gods or even Gentiles themselves, they become defiled. And they must enter into ritual washings just to be made right again." Clearly Marcus had done some study and was well prepared to advise Appius. "They also have numerous rules for food. But at least no rules for wine, unless you let insects swim in it." Here he laughed. "And you will have all the wine you want. And good wine at that. If we're in need of more supplies, Raphana is only a short distance away."

Appius's decision was firm. "Gaius will furnish our household as he always has. I will not accept a visit from Gallica and have them see that I've gone over to the Jewish religion. And we will tell the Jewish leaders they must adapt if they want to curry my favor. They will just take many baths! This may become the cleanest village in Galilee!" Appius clearly found it all amusing.

It took no time for the merchant with the villa to concede. These Romans were bringing fresh money to the village, and he was not going to miss out. Capernaum was small and poor. And while it was miserable to have the Romans on hand, still, they did bring money along with their pollutions. It was a compromise worth making.

Gaius drove the wagons directly to the villa and ordered the slaves in his charge to begin unloading everything they would need. He walked through the house, surveying what had to be done. It was austere, to be sure. The fountain in the center of the courtyard was broken and dry. There was a garden next to it, but it had been sorely neglected. It needed its own fountain, but that could wait. The inside of the walls had been plastered white,

SEA OF TIBERIUS

The Sea of Tiberius was the alternative name for the Sea of Galilee (see Jn 6:1). Antipas built the city of Tiberius to be his new capital. It was a beautiful lakeside town that he named after the reigning emperor, Tiberius. Soon the lake took the name as well. Today a thriving Israeli city of the same name is located here, but numerous ancient remains can be found at the city's southern entrance.

The sea is about fourteen miles long, north to south, and seven miles wide, east to west. Because it is in the Jordan River depression, it is seven hundred feet below sea level. The Jordan River flows into it at the north and exits at a southern outlet. As a freshwater lake, it was tremendously valuable as a source of fishing for the region.

giving the interior of the villa a cheerfulness not found elsewhere. Gaius not only wanted to make this place comfortable, but he knew that the happiness of Appius was critical to the security of all who lived there. He wanted Appius to live here—not in a fort—and in that living resolve again his commitment to his familia. Gaius did not want to see any erosion in that commitment. And the unspoken awkwardness with Tullus and Livia ran the risk of making it so.

Gaius set about taking notes on what needed to be purchased and how the rooms would be assigned. The front gate needed immediate repair because it held the security of the residence. Two soldiers with tools were called and arrived immediately to refit the hinges and the bolt on the inside. In very little time the villagers were gathering near the villa, offering their services for hire and any supplies they could sell. This was a poor village. Very poor. And they had not seen this much silver passing through their streets in a long time.

Tullus decided that his most useful service would be to help set up the household and organize a room for himself, where Appius's correspondence would take place and where he would meet with anyone that needed him. He was also very aware of Livia and where she was settling in. There was a spacious room on the far end of the courtyard that opened to the fountain through a small forecourt. She had chosen this for herself and Appius.

Each time Tullus moved through the central courtyard, he found himself glancing in Livia's direction. She was like an unresolved dream that he worked hard to hold on to, to reenter, but that he knew might easily slip away. But he was also wary. Appius returned to the villa regularly and unexpectedly. And Tullus's impulse was to conceal this dream as much as it was to explore it.

7

Capernaum

Gaius saw Livia's pregnancy as an omen. Whenever the gods gave fertility to a family, it meant rich blessing was on them. Gaius even found an oracle who was passing through the country and paid the woman to provide a prophecy. He was assured that the pregnancy was indeed an omen, a sign from the gods that all would be well. The oracle told Gaius that the gods were pleased with his master Appius and all his household.

Then she hesitated—for the slightest moment—and Gaius saw it. But the cloud seemed to pass, and the oracle repeated her glowing report.

Within a week the support troops from Caesarea had departed, and the small contingent of soldiers stationed in Capernaum had found permanent quarters on the edge of the village. However, Gaius noticed that Appius had decided to remain home. He seemed attached to his new villa and took pride in unpacking his collection. He even purchased a sculpture that he had seen in Caesarea and made it a centerpiece in the newly refurbished courtyard. The merchant said that it was a replica from Rome and extremely well done. It was a depiction of a deer desperately fighting for its life as five hunting dogs

ORACLES

The Greeks and Romans believed that the gods participated directly in human affairs. Their wishes could be known and their judgments understood. *Oracle* comes from the Latin meaning "to speak" (*orare*) and refers to priests or prophets generally located at temples where the gods could be consulted. The oracles at Delphi were perhaps the most famous oracles in the ancient world.

But there were others who had specialized knowledge of the gods' will, such as an augur. An augur was a person who could interpret the will of the gods by studying the flight of birds. These "seers" were very common throughout the Ro-

Figure 7.1. On the left in this wall painting an augur holding his symbolic curved wand is interpreting the meaning of the flight of birds

man era, and few major decisions were made without consulting them. Birds flew high in the sky, and since this was near to where the gods resided, their patterns could convey what they saw. Sometimes the augurs would listen to the sounds of birds and interpret them. When they examined birds, this was called reading the "auspices" (Latin *auspicium*, "bird watching"), and the report from them could either be good or bad (hence, our English terms *auspicious* and *inauspicious*).

savaged its body. Appius liked it. Tullus did not. In Tullus's mind the Roman comfort with violence was peculiar and disturbing.

Gaius also felt that the pregnancy was clarifying. It clarified Appius's attachment to Livia, particularly since Appius seemed genuinely pleased by her condition—otherwise he could have forced her to destroy it. Appius's pleasure also helped relieve Livia's anxiety. She had satisfied Appius and was contributing to the household. But, above all, the anticipated birth clarified Tullus's feelings toward Livia. He was unmistakably drawn to her—she knew it, Gaius knew it, and Appius suspected it. But Tullus now embraced this truth with courage: *Livia belongs to Appius. She is carrying his child.*

Eventually Tullus grew to be one of Livia's friends—someone she could confide in, someone able to understand her needs, something that Appius barely did.

Tullus now found that he had become a diplomat, standing between the leaders of Capernaum and Appius, whose diplomatic skills were untended. Tullus reminded himself that Appius was a soldier, and were it not for his injury, he would never take a post such as this. He wanted to be with the legion, but he had decided it was his good fortune to continue in service to the emperor even though he was incapable of fighting.

Tullus found that in Capernaum there were two audiences he needed to understand. There were the religious leaders of the village—elders, they called themselves—and there was a tax collector who had purchased the concession of tax collection from the provincial leaders in Caesarea some years ago. Both of these groups learned early that Tullus was Appius's most trusted assistant and that any successful connection to the Roman would have to come through this young man. The tax collector lived in Sepphoris and so was rarely available, except for his small band of men who were constantly registering property in the area.

The Jewish elders were the real managers of the village.

It was early in the first month in Capernaum that Tullus and Marcus met a delegation of Jewish elders approaching the villa. They were older men with full beards and long hair, wearing distinctive Jewish dress. Tullus found their appearance amusing, reminding him of the villagers in Emesa where he had grown up. Since he had joined Appius, however, Tullus had become "modern," and with Livia's help he had taken to wearing the newer togas. His hair was short, and he would never wear a beard.

"Welcome and peace be on you," said the man who clearly was the leader of this group. He bowed generously, as did each of the other three elders standing with him. They were speaking Greek with a heavy local accent. Many of their sentences were hardly Greek at all, but Tullus could piece together their intentions. In Emesa he had studied dialects as a part of his school curriculum. Now it served him well.

"We knew you were coming, and we are delighted to have you." The elders were working hard to make light talk, to ingratiate themselves, to build a bridge, it was apparent, and Tullus admired their efforts. Marcus seemed less receptive. He stood firmly with his arms folded.

"No bandits or thieves will dare step foot in Capernaum again!" At this each of them laughed, including Tullus. They all

CAPERNAUM

Capernaum (Hebrew *Kfar Nahum*, or "Nahum's Village") was a small fishing village on the north coast of the Sea of Galilee. And as a fishing village, it reflected the life of dozens of poor villages around this large freshwater sea. Villages in this area were especially fortunate, since freshwater springs

Figure 7.2. The remains of a first-century boat discovered in the mud of the Sea of Galilee in 1986

arise within the lake, and the fish are plentiful. A nearby site (first mentioned in the fourth century) is called Tabgah, from the Greek *heptapegon,* or "seven springs."

Ships netted fish daily, and these were pulled into holding ponds built adjacent to the village's harbor. Recently, when the level of the sea has been low during drought, researchers located the remains of these harbors not only at Capernaum but also elsewhere. One year the Israeli kibbutz Nof Ginosar discovered an ancient fishing vessel buried in the lakeshore sand. After intense study and effort, it was recovered and preserved. See jesusboat.com.

No doubt Capernaum was the most important of the villages along this Galilee coast. The main road that crossed through Galilee in this region ran through Capernaum. And this made it a convenient taxation point for Rome (Mt 9:9). This explains why there was a detachment of Roman soldiers in the village (Mt 8:5-9) and various officials representing regional rule (Jn 4:46). Jesus recognized the importance of the village as well. After his departure from Nazareth the village became the base of his own ministry in Galilee. In Matthew 9:1 Capernaum is referred to as "his own city" (ESV). Peter and Andrew (originally from Bethsaida, just east of the village) also lived there (Jn 1:44; Mk 1:29). Because Jesus frequented the village, many miracles were done there (cf. Mk 2:1-12), which led him to chide the city for its lack of faith given all that God had done for it (Mt 11:23).

The site (Arabic *Talhum*) had been abandoned for almost a thousand years and lay desolate. In the mid-nineteenth century a local Bedouin tribe (the Semekiyeh) camped on the site. But monumental ruins of what would turn out to be the synagogue were found on the surface; in 1894 and in 1894 the Franciscans purchased it, and excavations began in earnest. Today the first-century village has been uncovered, as well as a partially reconstructed fourth-century synagogue. This white limestone synagogue likely stands over a black basalt first-century synagogue that was the site of one of Jesus' first healings.

needed the moment of relief. But Marcus simply looked at them with apparent disdain.

Tullus knew that he could not invite them into the villa's public rooms or atrium. Marcus had told him of the Jewish objections to what they called idolatry. So, to avoid any awkwardness, Tullus did not extend an invitation. But through the gate the fearsome statue of the deer and the dogs was visible. The deer was defenseless and seemed as if it were screeching into the air as dogs hung from its neck. Tullus saw the elders look at the statue and register their disgust. And he wondered if his own thoughts were the same as theirs. *This is what Romans do. Who would erect such a thing in their household?* It did not help that the Jews viewed dogs as unclean.

"How can we help you settle in, my friends?"

"We have done well with our housing and our camp. But we will need better quarters for our troops." Marcus was well aware of the needs of the soldiers, and since this would be a long stay, he wanted to improve their situation.

"We have households that might be willing to part with rooms, for we are very poor people."

"And they will be poorer before we leave," Marcus quipped. "The needs of the emperor will determine where we live. Can we expect your full cooperation?"

Immediately they stiffened. Marcus had drawn a line and made clear that the Romans were not guests, they were conquerors. The awkward courtesies of the elders suddenly went cold.

"And what is your will with us in our land, young man?" One of the elders, who looked easily seventy, expressed no fear. He had a silver beard that Tullus thought made him look like a prophet. He stood erect and looked Marcus directly in the eye. Tullus noticed he was taller than Marcus. Almost forty years separated them.

"We own your land." Marcus seemed to be overreaching, asserting authority that was out of place, pushing these men, whom someday he may need as allies. Tullus knew things had taken a wrong turn.

"With all respect, God owns this land." Tullus was astonished at the elder's boldness. His voice did not waver. It was as if he made a pronouncement, seeming accustomed to audiences. He looked at the young Roman as he might an impertinent student.

THE DEER AND THE DOGS

This is a Roman sculpture that was found in the ruins of Herculaneum, a Roman city destroyed along with Pompeii in A.D. 79 when the volcano Vesuvius erupted. The sculpture is astonishing for the artistic skill of the sculptor and the violence of the image. It underscores the ease with which Romans welcomed such shocking scenes of cruelty in their homes.

Figure 7.3. First-century Roman statue of a deer attacked by dogs

The Jewish elders believed, as did their entire culture, that dogs were unclean. In this period they were scavengers, not pets, and could be used as negative examples. Even Jesus does this (Mt 7:6; 15:26). Paul too uses "dog" as a slur (Phil 3:2; compare 2 Pet 2:22; Rev 22:15). That Appius would give pride of place to a violent scene such as this would have been shocking to the elders.

At some level, Tullus admired him. The elder had no fear. He was not angry. He did not threaten any physical resistance. It was his will. Tullus thought his will was like granite. "And many who have come here before you with armies have found their grip on the land . . . well, uncomfortable. Difficult. But while you are here, you are most welcome." The elder did not flinch from Marcus's stare. His courtesies had now become weapons. Neither man moved. Only a slight breeze fluttered the elder's robes. Even his beard seemed to stiffen.

"Yours is no god we recognize or honor. Look around you, old man, and you will see that our gods have succeeded where your god has failed." Marcus was unnerving everyone, above all Tullus. *What in the world is Marcus thinking? Does he really think he speaks for Appius? For Rome?* Whatever Marcus's views, Tullus sensed with growing alarm that his own alliances were confused. He felt sympathy for the Jews and distrust for Marcus, the man to whom he had entrusted his life.

"We have been in this land over one thousand years. And you? You were born . . . when? And Rome was just a hill with some sheep—what, one hundred years ago?" The elder was willing to elevate this little war. Tullus knew it had to stop. He had seen Marcus's temper and his willingness to strike before he thought. Here in a remote village, where no one would know or report the rogue behavior of legionnaires, there was little restraining him.

"And has it never occurred to you why no soldiers have ever stayed in Capernaum permanently? And what happened to the last Gentiles who tried to occupy us? And what may happen to you?" Now it was the elder inflaming the tension, challenging Marcus, seeing whether he was capable of standing up to him.

"Perhaps you can show us the village," Tullus inserted. It was an odd thing to say, and he felt it was obvious that he was awkwardly trying to defuse the scene. But the only ones who welcomed the overture were the three silent elders, who looked truly frightened by how quickly things had fallen apart. Marcus and the other elder were squaring off. The elder could see the young man trying hard to assert himself, to prove he was in control. The elder had decided he didn't respect or fear him. But the elder would lose in this

JUDAS AND THE GREEK WARS

The Greek conquest of Judea came with the arrival of Alexander the Great and his armies in the fourth century B.C. This was followed by a series of Greek rulers, first from Egypt, then from Syria. By the second century B.C., the severity of their rule inspired a full rebellion called the Maccabean Revolt. The rebellion was led by the son of a priest named Judas son of Matthias, nicknamed Judas Maccabaeus ("Judas the Hammer"). Judas's successes against the Greeks were swift and led to the establishment of Jewish dynasties in Jerusalem by midcentury. However, internal divisions erupted within seventy-five years, and soon Jewish contingents were killing one another and sabotaging Jerusalem regularly. The conflict did not end until the Roman general Pompey conquered Judea in 63 B.C.

Figure 7.4. Alexander the Great

encounter, even though he had the greater stature.

"Seriously. Let us walk to the markets." Tullus stepped forward, while Marcus shot him an angry look. Tullus had robbed him of the moment that he wanted. So Marcus looked the elder over from head to toe, turned his back on him and began walking back to the Roman camp.

Tullus and the elders walked away from Appius's villa and soon found themselves near the coast of the lake, where families had set up small stalls and a variety of things were sold: foodstuffs, textiles, tools. Nearby were holding ponds for fish that had been netted and hauled in from the sea. Three small fishing vessels were tied up near the water's edge, moored by stone anchors. The main road that connected Capernaum to the rest of Galilee passed right before them.

The elder's tone and posture had relaxed once they left the villa. But Tullus understood: *This man hates the Romans and might well sabotage any efforts they make to control this place.*

"So how long have you lived here?" Tullus and the elder were walking ahead of the other elders. Everywhere they went, people stopped and stared. Tullus saw their looks not as springing from curiosity and welcome but as distancing, apprehensive. One woman reflexively pulled her child closer as they passed. Tullus didn't like being feared.

The elder stopped at the water's edge. "My family has been in Capernaum for many generations. My ancestors came here from Judea during the civil wars before the Romans arrived. They were escaping the terrors of Jerusalem."

"Civil wars?"

"When Jewish rule in Jerusalem was sovereign, after the defeat of the Greeks. When Judas led us to victory. But within a generation, families in Jerusalem were fighting for power. My fathers led us away, and so here we are in Galilee."

"And when Rome came, did they not put an end to the bloodshed? Do I not understand that Rome's conquest of Jerusalem was no conquest at all? But that the city was easily given over to them?"

"We traded freedom for safety. But at what price? Now Rome and its rulers take our wealth and strip us of our future. *And they profane the land. They profane the land!*" Tullus could see the elder rising to the moment again, ready to argue, but then deliberately bring himself down as he spoke:

"Behold, O Lord, and raise up for them their king, the Son of David, at the appointed time which you, O God, did choose, that he may reign over Israel your servant. And gird him with strength, that he may shatter unrighteous rulers, and may cleanse Jerusalem from the gentiles that trample her down in destruction. Wisely and righteously let him expel sinners from the inheritance, and destroy the sinner's pride as a potter's vessel. With a rod of iron may he break in pieces all their resources. Let him destroy the lawless gentiles by the word of his mouth" (*Pss. Sol.* 17:21-24).[1]

The elder paused and said, "But you speak of Rome as if she were your master, young one." Tullus suddenly reddened. He stopped walking. Without realizing it, he had spoken of the empire as not his own, as a force he served, as an army to which he too was subordinate.

He felt unmasked.

"You are not one of them, are you?" This was not the direction Tullus had wanted to take. He could not "side" with those whom Appius occupied. He could not become an ally of the army's enemy. He dare not betray Rome. Or Marcus.

---

[1]This translation is from R. P. Martin, *New Testament Foundations* (Grand Rapids: Eerdmans, 1975), 1:110-11.

UNCLEAN GENTILES

In our story Tobias represents a sentiment held strongly by the Jews of this era: the land of Judea was God's gift to them, and Gentiles, particularly the Romans, were making it impure simply by being there. The purity of Judea—preserved for one race, the children of Abraham—was the common basis of resistance to Rome as well as other invaders. In the *Psalms of Solomon*, written a century earlier, we have urgent prayers for the Messiah to cleanse Judea of "those who trample her down."

"You are different," the elder continued. "You do not share their love of power and war." He glanced back in the direction of the camp and Appius's villa. He then looked at the three silent elders, who nodded.

"What is your name? Your full name?"

Tullus was nervous. The elder was reaching out to him, connecting, closing some gap. The elder was in control of the conversation, and everything in Tullus screamed that he needed to be more Roman, more authoritative, wear his uniform as if he owned it.

"Tullus son of Onias, from Emesa in Syria." Tullus felt as if he had divulged a great secret. No one in Legion Gallica had asked him about Emesa. They had treated him as if he were nameless.

The elder leaned in uncomfortably close. He was looking in Tullus's eyes as if he could see through them. He seemed not to blink, and it was unnerving.

"Onias the oil trader?"

It was a moment Tullus would never forget, a moment set

apart from every other moment he had lived through. He had told no one about his father's occupation, not even Appius. *Does this elderly man know my father?* Tullus pushed these thoughts from his mind daily: that his family might be known, known even here and now. The destruction of Emesa was a dark thing he could not bear to revisit. It haunted him regularly, but above all, the fate of his family troubled him deeply.

"Yes. My father was a merchant, he traveled to Judea, and he sold to the markets in Syria and Phoenicia. But that was before the Romans destroyed Emesa." Tullus found his pulse rising, as if the elder held some secret, some knowledge that he desperately needed to hear. Nothing else mattered at that moment. Not Rome. Not Capernaum. Nothing else.

"Did you know my father?"

The elder seemed to be savoring the moment. He paused for what seemed an eternity. He seemed to know he was about to offer a gift, a sacred word that could transform this young man's world. "I *do know* Onias," he said. "And I know he is well. As is your mother. The people of Emesa—those who did not rebel—they escaped and are returning to their city and rebuilding it. And your father is among them."

Tullus rarely cried. But at once he was overcome, choking with a mixture of emotions he could barely comprehend: joy, relief, yearning, love. *His family was alive!* Now he could allow himself to think of a future. A future with them. A future that went beyond his assignments with Gallica and Appius. Suddenly Rome felt more distant, and he felt less attached. He was wearing the uniform of a foreigner.

The elder then reached out with both of his hands and clasped Tullus's shoulders. "And you are one of us, young Tullus. The blood of Abraham flows in your veins. Welcome home."

At this the elder embraced him. Without warning, the other

three did the same, and Tullus immediately was flooded with embarrassment, shame and shock. His family did not talk about this. His father never practiced this faith, though Tullus vaguely knew that their "tribe" came from this region. But other tribes lived in Emesa, and Tullus's father always said that such origins made little difference. Their family observed some of the rituals of the Jews, but so did many other Syrians and Greeks living in Emesa. Tullus was incredulous. *I am one of these people that I have been sent to help rule.* And at once, he knew: this was a secret he had to keep from every Roman he knew.

As Tullus and the elder, who now introduced himself as Tobias, laughed and talked along with the other three elders, a courier interrupted the men. He was a soldier who worked at the villa with Appius. He was out of breath and was carrying desperate news—his face betrayed him.

Tullus immediately gathered himself and instinctively disguised any familiarity or intimacy he had with these men. He immediately became Roman, just as Appius had mentored him.

"Tullus." The man was breathing heavily. Marcus had required that the men wear much of their battle gear when they entered the village.

"Appius sent me. It's Livia. Something is wrong with her. There is blood. And Appius fears she will not only lose her child but lose her life. He wants to know whether there are physicians in this place."

"Do we not have a physician apprentice among our men?"

"No. We have none. Appius is afraid. *Tullus, Livia may die.*"

Tullus turned to Tobias and the other elders in desperation. He too was afraid. Not only for what this death would mean for Appius, but what this would mean for him.

"Follow me." Tobias took Tullus by the arm and began walking quickly through the narrow lanes of the village.

8

Capernaum's Midwife

Tobias was not simply an elder among the Jews of Capernaum; he was *the elder* presiding over the community. He resolved complaints, made judgments on inheritances, reconciled neighbors and, as the most literate man in the village, he was the local authority on matters of religious law. But Tobias also had strong sentiments when it came to the land and its occupation. He was not interested in compromise with the Romans—and he felt the Jewish leaders in Jerusalem were too often complicit in Rome's hold on the nation. He believed firmly in the Messiah and was convinced that when Messiah came, he would bring deliverance from Gentile occupation and ignite a revival of Israel's life.

Rome had offered peace—the Pax Romana—but the price was subjugation to Roman military rule. Tobias believed that God alone could give peace, but it would appear only when righteousness returned, when God's reign resumed in Judea, and the law was obeyed. God's faithfulness to his people never wavered. But their faithfulness to him often did.

Tobias also knew the families of Capernaum better than anyone. And he knew immediately where to go to seek help for Livia.

Tullus, Tobias, the camp courier and the other elders cut a swift path through the village until they arrived at the small house of a man known as a practitioner of healing. He was lettered and had an excellent knowledge of laws pertaining to health and recovery. He and Tobias consulted regularly, especially in matters of hygiene, because both believed—the Torah taught them—that the regulation of hygiene (the separation of the ill; the washing of wounds and so on) was God's means of preserving them. But they were also clear: it was God alone who brought healing when they needed it. Any other remedy using potions or incantations was magic. *And the healer did not practice magic.*

In the street Tobias prompted the soldier to retell what he knew. The healer and his wife—both elderly—listened carefully and glanced at each other frequently, comparing conclusions. The woman, Tullus learned, was the village midwife.

"She is with child?" the physician asked.

"She is but has barely begun to show," Tullus answered.

"Did you say this is a Roman woman?" Tullus flinched, not liking how the physician asked the question or that he thought it mattered.

"She is," Tobias said. "And she is with the centurion." Tobias saw the healer take a step back. His interest in the case had visibly diminished.

"And you, Tobias, would have me enter there and offer help?" the physician asked.

"Not to do so would be to invite his anger," Tobias said. "I do not like it any more than you, but we must think about the village. This man has the power to help us or destroy us."

"And to come near her, to enter their household, would render us all unclean. *I do not help Romans.*"

At this the physician's wife, the village midwife, stepped into the middle of the men. She spoke with anger and a barely veiled disgust. "None of this matters. A young woman needs us and so we go. Her name is Livia? We are walking. Now."

Looking at Tobias, she spoke with her finger pointed: "And do not even mention anything to me about idols or Gentiles, Tobias."

"But, Mariam, there is the matter of the law. . . ."

"And there is what must be done! You men may discuss this for all I care. I am going to tend to her care. And I will not talk about it."

Reaching into the doorway of her home, she picked up a small

IDOLATRY AND THE JEWS

Based on the second commandment ("You shall not make for yourself an image in the form of anything in heaven above or on the earth beneath or in the waters below," Ex 20:4), Jews prohibited the construction of sculptured images, which they termed idols. This was a constant area of conflict from the Old Testament era right through the Greek and Roman periods, when idols were commonplace. That Appius has a collection of statues of Apollo would not be surprising. Nor would it surprise anyone that Tobias found them abhorrent.

Even the early Christians had to struggle with this. Jewish Christians found Roman idolatry offensive, and they asked Gentile Christians to avoid "food polluted by idols" (Acts 15:20). Paul refers to idols frequently and describes conversion to Christ as turning "from idols to serve the living and true God" (1 Thess 1:9).

birthing stool and immediately began walking briskly in the direction of the villa. The men abruptly ended their theological discussion about Gentiles and purity before it could reach full bloom. Tullus struggled to keep pace with the midwife, ready to give directions, while an entourage of men followed: Tobias, three village elders and the village healer. The young Roman courier followed alone at the rear.

When they arrived at the villa's gate, Gaius was waiting for them. A look of desperation and panic creased his face. He was facing something he could not control. And Gaius was rarely not in control.

As Tullus and the midwife had approached the villa, it was evident that the men following them were slowing down. They had committed themselves to separation and resistance as long as Rome dwelt in this land. So when they reached the gate, the midwife immediately turned on her heel and stared directly at her husband, who had planted himself some distance away with Tobias. She said nothing. Nor did she have to. Almost immediately he stepped away from Tobias and joined her as they discussed with Gaius what had happened.

Gaius led them into the inner courtyard and directly to the far rooms where Appius and Livia slept. Tullus had not yet visited this side of the villa, but now, with the physician and his wife at his side, he felt he had license. Gaius, Tullus and the two Jewish healers soon were at the door, where Appius greeted them.

"She is stricken by fever," Appius said, "and talks about terrible pain. . . ."

Mariam saw the bed across the room and walked in even as Appius was still talking. There she found Livia, pale and trembling in fear. Her bedclothes were soaked with sweat. There was blood on the bed linens.

Placing her wrinkled hands on either side of Livia's face, Mariam spoke gently but directly as the young woman focused.

"My name is Mariam and you are Livia. Do you understand me, Livia?" Livia nodded. "Tell me what you feel."

Tullus was amazed how quickly Mariam took charge of the scene. Within moments she was giving orders. Even her husband was watching in amazement.

FEVER

Throughout the Roman era and until quite recently, fever was not understood to be a consequence of some other disease or injury. Fever was a disease of its own and had to be treated separately. For any who were schooled in Greek or Roman medical academies, the problem was one of imbalance. When the body overheated, heat was in the blood, which needed to be released to restore balance.

Mariam does not attempt this but instead uses hygiene and food to strengthen Livia. Hot water scented with cinnamon was a common medicinal beverage. In the ancient world scents or aromas were understood to have strong medicinal effects.

"We need room in here. Leave us and wait outside." Mariam's eyes quickly scanned the growing crowd of men. Then she looked to Tullus. "Bring me hot water and cinnamon. And oil mixed with myrrh. This woman needs to be bathed and readied. And bring me linen. As much linen as you can find." Tullus ran from the room to collect his assignments. Appius ushered the men into the courtyard.

Mariam studied Livia as she began to remove Livia's bedclothes. "You are birthing, my dear. But the child is not formed."

Livia shuddered. "Do not be afraid. I have seen many of these and you will be well." Livia began looking about the room aimlessly, her eyes unfocused.

"Livia, look at me." Mariam spoke directly into her face, holding her again. "Are you afraid?" Livia nodded, while Mariam continued with a voice like that of a centurion. "I am not afraid. Look at me, Livia. I know what must be done. I will not leave you this day, Livia. *I will not lose you.*"

Livia began to cry but never stopped looking into Mariam's eyes. "Repeat these words with me, Livia. 'I am the Lord who heals you.' Say this with me." As Mariam spoke words from her Scriptures, Livia began to repeat them. With each repetition, strength and confidence seemed to return to her.

Tullus appeared shortly and found Mariam now moving Livia to the side of the bed and then on to her birthing stool. He handed Mariam everything she requested and then backed quietly from the room to join Appius and the others outside. Mariam and her husband had matters well in hand.

The wait in the courtyard seemed interminable. The men stood looking at the floor. They could hear Livia cry out again and again, while Mariam's steady voice continued in reassuring words and tone. Still, Appius's fear would not be eased. As time wore on, he aimlessly wandered in the villa's neglected garden, even taking an interest in examining the stones laborers were collecting for a new fountain.

Much of the day wore on like this. Mariam's husband would emerge and ask for more oil or water. And then he would disappear again. Finally Mariam stepped from the room and spoke directly to Appius. "You have lost your child. But God has been good and he has saved its mother. Livia has been bathed and cleaned and is now stronger. She must remain in bed for three to four days and do no work. Come for me if anything is amiss.

But I shall return in the morning to check on her."

An expression of gratitude was on Appius's lips, but the woman was quickly gathering her things and readying her departure. She was done. She left as directly as she had arrived. They walked toward the gate, and Mariam looked quickly at the statues and sculptures in Appius's collection. When she saw the dogs and the deer, Tullus thought he saw her close her eyes and shake her head.

Tullus escorted Mariam and her husband to the gate, and after a moment's hesitation, he asked if he might walk with them back into the village.

The two of them nodded. "You did well today, Tullus," Mariam offered. "I can see that Livia trusts you."

"Thank you. Both of you. You saved our household today."

"Give God the praise, young man. We do little compared to him. I have seen women die in such times as this. And when they are saved, it is God who saves them."

Here she stopped. And she looked directly at Tullus in a way that made him apprehensive. "Did you pray for her?" Tullus was stunned. No one had spoken like this to him before about religion.

"No. I do not know how."

"I learned today that you are one of us, Tullus. Is this true?"

"It is."

"Is this a secret?" Mariam's look seemed severe, and Tullus hoped it was sincerity.

"I have told no one in my household."

"So you should know how to pray and who it is that answers prayer, Tullus. And it is not any of those idols in that house. They are useless. But you belong to a God who is alive. Do not forget this, young Tullus."

"And my secret?"

MIDWIVES

Most of the villages in the Roman world had midwives who oversaw women's pregnancies and births. We should assume that such women tended to Mary at Jesus' birth, even though they are not mentioned. Birthing was always done at home, and it was considered a very dangerous passage for a woman (see 1 Tim 2:15). During Livia's miscarriage, Mariam uses the Scripture to help Livia focus. This text, "I am the Lord, who heals you," is from Exodus 15:26.

Roman medical writers wrote extensively about childbirth and the qualifications of a midwife. In the second century A.D., a famous Roman physician named Soranus of Ephesus penned, "A suitable person will be literate, with her wits about her, possessed of a good memory, loving work, respectable and generally not unduly handicapped as regards her senses [i.e., sight, smell, hearing], sound of limb, robust, and, according to some people, endowed with long slim fingers and short nails at her fingertips." Soranus also said that the midwife should be of sympathetic disposition (though she need not herself have borne a child) and keep her hands soft, so she would not cause discomfort to either mother or child.[a]

Figure 8.1. A woman giving birth on a birth stool

[a]*Soranus' Gynecology*, trans. Owsei Temkin (Baltimore: The Johns Hopkins University Press, 1956), 1.2.4. See also P. M. Dunn, "Soranus of Ephesus (circa A.D. 98-138) and Perinatal Care in Roman Times," *Archives of Disease in Childhood: Fetal and Neonatal* 73, no. 1 (July 1995): F51-F52.

"It will remain so. You must watch after this young woman. Make sure she eats and especially drinks as much as she can. She has lost much blood, and she will be weak. You can do this, but I am less sure about the other men in that household."

With this, Mariam turned and walked toward her house, her husband following.

For days Appius went in and out of Livia's room, pacing the floor, looking for signs of healing. Mariam arrived every morning. And from the first day Gaius learned that when she was attending to Livia, he was expected to busy himself with other things. Tullus looked after Livia's welfare as well, but Gaius quickly took charge of her care and made it clear that Tullus ought to have other duties to attend to. He preferred that Tullus stay away from this side of the villa. After four days Livia seemed improved.

Appius was more relieved by the day. And relief brought with it ambivalent feelings about the Jews. Marcus did not trust them and implied that loyalty to Rome required a degree of distance from them, even a practiced hostility. He once commented, "You cannot favor those whom you rule. Or they will turn this favor into advantage." It sounded like a quote from a military manual. And while Appius nodded at this, still, he was impressed with how the Jewish community, particularly Mariam, had stepped into Livia's crisis and helped. He was grateful, though he wasn't sure that was a good thing. He was in control. Still, perhaps he could wed gratefulness with control. Perhaps this could be seen as diplomacy, advancing Rome's interests, while also offering thanks for their care.

These conflicted feelings gave birth to an assignment for Tullus. "Find out from this community what I can do for them. They have helped us. We may need this help again. Learn what they need, and as a token, perhaps we may provide it. Livia

THE PAX ROMANA

The Roman republic ended with the assassination of Julius Caesar in 44 B.C., and this led to tremendous civil war in the empire. A general named Octavian rose to power, defeated the opponents of Julius Caesar and was hailed by the senate as "Caesar Augustus," son of the divine Julius. Augustus became the first "emperor" of this period and ruled from 27 B.C. to A.D. 14.

Figure 8.2. A Roman coin with an image of Augustus Caesar on one side, and *pax*, "peace," on the other

Augustus needed to restore the empire. He launched a number of aggressive programs and promised that the Pax Romana ("Peace of Rome") would return to the empire. He promised economic prosperity, military security and domestic order. He defeated the pirates of the Mediterranean and secured trade routes. Then he built the largest army the world had ever seen. And, finally, he pursued the restoration of the order of the Roman family (familia). Augustus claimed this agenda would only work if every Roman and every conquered province gave its complete loyalty to the empire. The propaganda enforcing these ideals could be seen on coins, monuments, publications and temples throughout the Mediterranean.

In villages like Capernaum, the Romans brought both promise and captivity. On the one hand, the tyranny of Roman rule guaranteed a degree of stability and security, freedom from much banditry, and the prospect of economic development for the upper classes. On the other hand, it came with a price: heavy taxation and severe penalties for resistance. The poor on the fringes of the empire never benefited from the Pax Romana. It was a promise of peace for those who lived within the mainstream of Roman society and those of high stature in the provinces who joined the Roman imperial project.

would not still be with us were it not for Mariam. I shall not forget her kindness."

Ever since the day Tullus had met Tobias, the young scribe felt drawn to the Jewish community of Capernaum. He wanted to learn more, to explore what he had missed in his early years, to discover what it meant to be Jewish.

On the fifth day after Livia's loss, Tobias invited Tullus to meet with the elders at his home. They would have a meal after dusk—something they did regularly—and Tullus was their guest. However, he did not want to be a spectacle.

It was dusk when Tullus arrived at Tobias's modest home. He could see a gathering of about a dozen men. A low table was set up in the courtyard with cushions set around it. Tobias spotted Tullus and quickly walked over to the gate. He kissed Tullus generously, as if they were long-lost friends, and pulled him toward the lamp-lit table and its spread of food. There were mounds of fresh bread, olives, fruit from many trees, and a fish stew that seemed to be a staple in the village.

A JEWISH *HAVERIM*

Devout Jews created voluntary associations in this era called *Haverim* (from Hebrew *haver* or *chaver,* "friend"). We think they met regularly for meals and discussed the law but also committed one another to purity and obedience to the law. Tobias, as a devout teacher of the law, is likely hosting such a gathering at his home. The meal would be followed by an exposition of the law, and then a lively discussion would ensue. In this case, Tobias reads from Psalm 17. Some scholars think that these *Haverim* met multiple times each week.

Jesus grew up knowing such gatherings well. It is likely that he gathered with men such as this throughout his adolescence and young adulthood and learned to debate the law and its application well before he began his ministry.

Throughout his adult ministry Jesus was likely invited to many *Haverim*. We have one account that describes it fully in Luke 7:36-50. Note that the men are reclining, not sitting, at low tables and are surrounded by cushions. Eating was done using bread as a utensil, and common dishes were shared.

"Young Tullus, come in, come in. We have much to discuss." A servant helped remove Tullus's sandals and washed his feet. As Tobias led him into the gathering of men, Tullus felt overwhelmed and wanted to retreat. *What am I doing here? If Appius knew of this . . .* Tobias took his arm and led him to the table where the other men were standing, waiting for Tobias to recline. "Sit here, Tullus, next to me, so we can talk." All eyes were on them, curious how this young man dressed as a Roman was enjoying such a seat of honor.

After Tobias offered a word of blessing, bowls of cool water were passed around for washing. Soon everyone was drinking red wine from expertly carved stone cups.

Plates and bowls circulated, and Tobias took bread, tore it

Figure 8.3. A wall painting of a triclinium, an arrangement for reclining while dining

GALILEAN STONEWARE

Jews carefully monitored which materials were susceptible to impurity, or ritual uncleanness (Hebrew *taharah*). The second-century compilation of oral laws (the Mishnah) has an entire section devoted to "impurities."[a] Domestic items such as bowls and cups made of pottery were deemed to be susceptible to impurity,[b] and if something unclean, such as an insect, landed on a pottery vessel, it had to be broken and its contents discarded. However, items made from stone

Figure 8.4. Examples of Galilean stoneware

were not susceptible.[c] But, being carved entirely from one piece of stone, they were expensive. Nevertheless stoneware was used widely in the first century by those committed to purity.

Archaeologists have discovered significant quantities of stoneware throughout Israel where first-century Jewish communities have been excavated. Near Sepphoris the remains of what appears to have been a stone utensil factory have been discovered.

This explains Tobias's use of stoneware at his table. He is a devout Jew, likely a Pharisee, and deeply committed to purity law.

---

[a]Mishnah Order 6, *Tohorot.*
[b]Lev 11:33; Mishnah *Kelim* 2-10.
[c]Mishnah *Kelim* 10:1.

and, accompanied by his rich laughter, handed half to Tullus. Together they used the bread to dig into the fish stew that was steaming on the table. Figs, olives and spicy fish sauce circulated generously as the men talked and laughed, and in some corners enjoyed mild arguments about village matters. Tullus listened and felt strangely at home. It was a feeling he had never experienced in Gallica. Or in Appius's own household.

When the meal was winding down, the men looked to Tobias to open its next chapter. He reached for a scroll and, opening it, read aloud:

> My steps have held to your paths;
> my feet have not stumbled.
> I call on you, my God, for you will answer me;
> turn your ear to me and hear my prayer.
> Show me the wonders of your great love,
> you who save by your right hand
> those who take refuge in you from their foes.
> Keep me as the apple of your eye;
> hide me in the shadow of your wings
> from the wicked who are out to destroy me,

from my mortal enemies who surround me.
They close up their callous hearts,
and their mouths speak with arrogance.
They have tracked me down, they now surround me,
with eyes alert, to throw me to the ground.
They are like a lion hungry for prey,
like a fierce lion crouching in cover.

After the reading there was silence. Tobias began to explain what this text from the Psalms meant. When he was done, the room erupted into a cacophony of noise, as debate flew from every quarter. *How do we keep ourselves on the right path? Is God's faithfulness awaiting our righteousness? What will God do to save us? Who are our enemies who surround us? Should we act to defeat them or should we wait on God?*

Tobias, in the lowest of whispers, interpreted to Tullus what it all meant. Some of the men were waiting on God for their redemption; others believed that redemption required taking action. Moses' confrontation with Pharaoh was a favorite metaphor. "And if Moses had done nothing, we would be eating this bread in Egypt tonight!" they protested. Tullus wondered whether the men were being discreet for his sake. *Is Rome the mortal enemy that the Jewish God will defeat? Is Rome the fierce lion, the implacable enemy who loves violence and conquest? Do some of these men want to fight Appius? Do I belong to the wrong side?*

Tobias raised his hand, and the table was silenced. "We need to hear from Tullus, my friends." Tullus was petrified. He could not, would not, comment on a passage like this. What was Tobias thinking?

"Tullus, tell us your story. Tell us about your home in Emesa. Tell us about your life. We want to know you."

Tullus was stunned. Here were at least a dozen men and a

handful of servants, each staring at him, leaning in, eager to hear his every word. Never had he been given this honor by the Romans. The oil lamps arrayed on the table were reflecting in

JEWISH RESISTANCE

Jewish leadership agreed that the Roman occupation (just like that of the Greeks earlier) was offensive and needed to end. But how this would happen was hotly disputed. And the debate around Tobias's table is representative. Should they fight the Romans with weapons? Should they wait for God to intervene? Should they separate themselves from all contact with Rome? Or should they collaborate in order to make their life better and perhaps win more freedom?

Even Jesus' political outlook was tested. In Mark 12:13-17 some of the leaders asked him whether they should pay the imperial tax to Caesar. This was a thinly veiled test. It was less about taxes and chiefly about resistance. Should Jews cooperate with Rome or resist?

each man's eyes, while shadows played on the walls of the courtyard. It was unnerving. The room was silent. Tullus heard crickets outside. The wicks on the oil lights spit and hissed as the oil burned on their fringes.

Tullus began with his capture, his service for Legion Gallica in the household of Appius, their many campaigns, and finally arrived at the disaster in Dura-Europos. He went on to tell about how Appius was reassigned to Capernaum, but he did not mention Appius's problem with his arm. He emphasized how good Appius's household had been to him. He painted rich pictures of their household members: the slaves, Gaius who directed them, Livia, and even the present company of soldiers who lived in the town. "They are here simply to oversee the tax collection, and that is all," he urged. But few were convinced.

"And why should we pay taxes at all?" a voice queried from a darker corner.

Tobias immediately shot a look so severe that the question was dead on arrival. Tullus would not be interrogated.

"And you, Tullus. How does it feel to be a Jew and now serving this empire?" Tobias was trying to be diplomatic, but even he did not seem to be able to help asking a faintly pointed question.

"I do not know. I simply know that I am grateful to be here. I never expected the open hand each of you has given me. And yet I also know that my fate would have been far worse if a centurion other than Appius had taken me. And I tell you this, too. Your fate will be different if another replaces Appius. There are other legionnaires who are severe and cruel. Appius is neither of these. He is a good man who treats his household with honor. And he will do the same for you."

"And how can we be sure of this, Tullus? There are some outside this room who would do violence to these soldiers." Tobias was looking directly at him, and everyone waited for his answer.

"Perhaps some contribution, some exchange of gifts, something that will show good will on both sides. Through the hands of Mariam you saved Livia, the woman of Appius's household. He has not forgotten. And so I ask: What gift would you receive from Appius?"

"Our freedom!" shouted a voice, and everyone laughed. Tobias took it as good humor and held his hand aloft for more silence.

"Perhaps he could help this poor village with something it has never had." Tobias was thinking.

"Anything, Tobias. Give me an idea, and I am sure I can make it so."

"A synagogue." At this, the room fell into an even deeper silence. Surrounding villages larger than Capernaum each had houses of gathering where prayers could be said, meetings held, and a small school established. "We meet in homes during the winter and under the olive trees during the summer. *But we have never had a house of prayer*. Could he help us build one?"

Tobias resisted the temptation to mention that the centurion could use some of *their* own money that he collected.

"A house of prayer?" Tullus began to think about it. He knew that Appius had surplus money. He had heard him talk about it on many occasions. The cost of his latest sculpture would alone lay the foundation for such a building.

Tullus looked around the room. "I think this could happen."

9

Capernaum's Synagogue

Appius was intrigued by Tullus's recommendation. He explained it to Marcus and the other soldiers as a means of winning the support of the Jews in Capernaum. "A diplomatic overture," Appius said. Most, however, thought otherwise. Particularly Marcus. Appius had softened, and the episode with Livia and Mariam had yielded an unpredicted result. Appius had begun to view the Jews differently. Marcus found this worrisome.

In the same week that Tullus brought the recommendation to him, Appius hosted a man he was eager to meet: a tax collector of western Galilee named Chuza. Marcus had done some research on him: he was a Jew related to the Herodian family ruling western Galilee, a cousin of Herod Antipas, perhaps. He and his wife, Joanna, lived in Sepphoris (in his new palace on the Sea of Tiberius) and were enormously wealthy. He was the chief financial steward handling the budgets for Herod's region, but apparently he had his own tax business on the side. He had purchased the right to collect Rome's taxes around Capernaum, and it was proving profitable. For the most part everyone in Capernaum despised Chuza. He paid the tax bill Rome required of the region, but he also took profits over and above whenever he could by charging surpluses. The system was rife with corruption.

Chuza traveled with a small entourage of assistants and guards. There were ten of them, and they all arrived on horseback. Gaius met them at the gate, and Appius greeted them in the courtyard, formally and with reserve. The Romans wore their finest uniforms, and Gaius served wine and cuisine that befit the status they wanted to convey.

"Chuza, peace to you. You have traveled far. Let my servants care for your men while we talk." Soon wine, pears and figs, many cheeses, bread and seasoned fish on platters were circulating among the men as they admired Appius's rebuilt garden, his statues and the decorations on the walls now under way. Appius and Chuza, followed by their personal assistants, walked to the meeting room, where Livia awaited with even more expensive fare. Appius was clearly delighted to see how beautiful and vibrant she looked. She seemed to have strongly recovered. Chuza noticed her as well.

"So I see you are well settled into one of our little villas." Chuza spoke to Appius while looking at Livia, clearly seeking an opening with her. Tullus noted it immediately. Chuza kept scanning the room, sizing up what Appius had done with the place.

"Indeed. We have a good company of men, they have a camp nearby, and we are in regular communication with Legion Gallica in Raphana. And the village has welcomed us."

"The village. This is a useless place, and so poor that it barely pays us. It is the way station that counts here. Trade moves through Capernaum from both north and south, and if caravans pass through the district, they must pay. I have men working here, and they will look to you for reinforcement. They will tell you what they need." Tullus was surprised. *Did this man just give Appius an order?*

CHUZA OF SEPPHORIS

Luke 8:2-3 refers to wealthy Galileans who financially supported the ministry of Jesus. Here we learn about a woman named Joanna and her friend Susanna, who helped finance Jesus' ministry. Luke adds that Joanna's husband, named Chuza, "was the financial steward of Herod." From this we can surmise: Chuza worked for Herod Antipas in west Galilee, handling his financial affairs. He likely lived either in Sepphoris or Antipas's new city of Tiberius (on the Sea of Galilee), and possibly had no idea that his wife was aiding a Jewish prophet that Antipas himself suspected to be a danger to his rule. Chuza was no doubt wealthy, and in this story he is the "tax collector" (sometimes called "tax farmers") of the Capernaum district.

Figure 9.1. Provincial coins struck by Herod Antipas of Galilee

This means that Chuza would have purchased the privilege of collecting taxes for Rome as an investment. Once he submitted to Herod Antipas what was due from the province, he could keep the surplus. In other words, he could exceed

> the formally assessed tax amount as a return on his own investment. It goes without saying that such a system led to enormous corruption and tax oppression among the poor.
>
> Chuza indicates that he has "men working for him" as tax collectors. In Matthew 9:9 we learn one of their names. He is Matthew, whom Jesus will call away from his work and make an apostle (he is also called Levi, Mk 2:14). Matthew will write our Gospel by that name.

"Rome has sent me here to ensure the collection of taxes and the stability of the region," Appius said. "I trust that you are contributing to both equally." Appius had read his tone correctly and returned the volley. Chuza smiled and continued to look at Livia. Appius told her to leave the room.

"I care about one thing," Chuza said. "And that is the cooperation of this district. But you should know this, Appius. The district is not peaceful. There are many who would rebel, and we have seen a number of rebellions thus far. The echo of the rebel Judas the Galilean over twenty years ago still rings in these hills. There are always prophets and self-appointed messiahs who claim that God is leading them to restore Jewish rule on their terms. A man named John surfaced not long ago, and Antipas had him killed. He was an arrogant meddler in Antipas's personal life. No one was surprised at what happened to him. Even his followers admire martyrdom."

"And has this stopped the rebellions?"

"No. These people produce prophets endlessly. Even today there is a man from Nazareth who moves from village to village claiming to be yet another one of them. We watch him closely, and so should you."

JOHN THE BAPTIST

Chuza is referring to John the Baptist, whose prophetic ministry criticized the marriage of Herod Antipas to his brother's wife, Herodias. Antipas ruled not only western Galilee but the east shore of the Jordan River all the way to the Dead Sea (then called Perea). Therefore John the Baptist was within Antipas's rule. The Gospel of Mark tells the full story of Antipas's anxiety about John the Baptist (Mk 6:14-29), how he had the prophet beheaded and how he worried that in some manner Jesus was empowered by the resurrected Baptist who had returned to haunt him.

Any Roman or Jewish ruler in Galilee would have viewed the popular following of both John the Baptist and Jesus with considerable suspicion. John spoke openly about the corruption of the Jewish leadership and targeted Herod Antipas of Galilee in particular. His criticism of the Jerusalem leadership was equally harsh. "But when he saw many of the Pharisees and Sadducees coming for baptism, he said to them, 'You brood of vipers! Who warned you to flee from the coming wrath? Produce fruit in keeping with repentance. And do not think you can say to yourselves, "We have Abraham as our father." I tell you that out of these stones God can raise up children for Abraham. The ax is already at the root of the trees, and every tree that does not produce good fruit will be cut down and thrown into the fire'" (Mt 3:7-10). These sentiments echo the attitudes of the sectarian Jews who lived at Qumran near the Dead Sea. They too were committed to a purity of faith only found in the desert and were deeply suspicious of those who held institutional religious power.

"Has he ever entered Capernaum?"

"Yes. And you need to know his language is cleverly political. He gathers large crowds and talks openly about his own kingdom. His soldiers are these peasants you find in every village."

"Surely not all these people are as you think."

"Most are. Which is why you are here. Your sword is all we need. It is what your commanders require. I know them well and have discussed your assignment here with them already. I am sure they look to your success . . . our success. We speak to them in Caesarea regularly."

Appius's dislike for this man was clearly growing. He led every conversation with entitlement and presumption. Worse yet, he seemed to view Appius as working for him. His reference to Caesarea was offensive, and Appius wouldn't stand for it.

"And your success, Chuza? You assume that your interests are the same as Rome. Am I wrong?" Appius began to press Chuza's assumptions. "Perhaps the sword is not the only means of pacifying a village."

"It is the only language they understand."

"Look. Do you want my support or not? I am the only military unit in this district, and if you want protection from rebels, you need what I have."

Chuza felt the change in tone and paused. "And what do you offer?"

"But it will come on my terms, Chuza. I can have a cohort here in days, but you have nothing but a small band of untested fighters. Do not think you can demand Rome to serve your bidding. My commanders in Caesarea and Raphana have the fullest trust in me. And for you to meddle in my affairs will not serve you well."

Appius walked across the room and slowly removed Chuza's wine chalice from his hand, setting it on a table. "You enter my

JUDAS THE GALILEAN (FROM GAMLA)

Judas the Galilean was one of many Jewish rebels who resisted Roman rule in the first century. First-century Jewish historian Josephus refers to him (*Antiquities* 18.4-5, 23), as does the New Testament (Acts 5:37). Such men led uprisings inspired by a theocratic nationalism, claiming that God alone was the true ruler of Judea and that the Romans must be expelled. They opposed Roman taxation as a form of slavery, assumed that God would speedily come to their aid and had no fear of martyrdom. Josephus's description: "Yet there was one Judas . . . of a city whose name was Gamla, who . . . became zealous to draw them to a revolt, who both said that this taxation was no better than an introduction to slavery, and exhorted the nation to assert their liberty."

Judas's revolt took place in A.D. 6, and it was crushed violently by Rome and served as a Roman warning to any subsequent leaders who might try to do the same.

What did leaders such as Judas read for inspiration? Certainly the conquests of Joshua contributed to their confidence. But particularly the defeat of the Greeks in the Maccabean era (second century B.C.) modeled how the Romans could be defeated. They did not have to go far into their own contemporary writings to find a religious militancy fully displayed. The first-century B.C. *Psalms of Solomon* offers a prayer for conquest that dreams of purifying Judea of all Gentiles:

"Behold, O Lord, and raise up for them their king, the

Son of David, at the appointed time which you, O God, did choose, that he may reign over Israel your servant. And gird him with strength, that he may shatter unrighteous rulers, and may cleanse Jerusalem from the gentiles that trample her down in destruction. Wisely and righteously let him expel sinners from the inheritance, and destroy the sinner's pride as a potter's vessel. With a rod of iron may he break in pieces all their resources. Let him destroy the lawless gentiles by the word of his mouth" (*Pss. Sol.* 17:21-24).[a]

---

[a]Translation from R. P. Martin, *New Testament Foundations* (Grand Rapids: Eerdmans, 1975), 1:110-11.

household, you drink my wine, and you demand that I pour more. It is Rome that gives you everything you have. With a simple order, Legion Gallica could march on your city of Sepphoris and destroy it in days." Appius stepped closer. "This village is under my command, and for you to jeopardize it will put your own master Herod Antipas in jeopardy with Rome."

Chuza seemed astonished at Appius's abrupt shift. He looked to his assistants, who stood nervously nearby. Marcus stepped closer to the conversation to be visible—and it was clear that he was a man that did not like talk.

"And what do you think might pacify this village, Appius?"

"We are going to make a start by giving them a gift and obligating them to obedience." Appius was smiling, knowing how unexpected this idea might be.

"We are going to make these villagers value our rule and see Rome as their savior. This is the Roman way throughout the empire, from Spain to Syria, and it is evident that you who live in these remote hills do not understand it." The last words were meant to sting, and Tullus saw they had hit their mark.

Appius folded his arms and began what sounded like a lecture. "Rome wants *allies*, not mere subjects. If they choose not to be allies, then we will devastate them. But they require a choice first. We will trade: safety and security for their loyalty. And you watch: this bargain will win them. Judea and Syria belong to us, but if Persia should attack these regions, we do not want these people turning against us without cause. And you, Chuza, would cause the very rebellions you try to suppress."

Appius now called Tullus to his side, but the scribe had no idea what was about to happen. "We have a project, and you will join it. We are going to build Capernaum's first public building. Not a basilica or a temple—but something modest. We will lay the foundation for their religious house. I will pay for its foundation, and you will pay for its walls. If, of course, you wish my support."

"I have never heard—"

"We need discuss it no further," Appius interrupted. He asked Tullus for the amounts that would be needed, which Tullus made up on the spot. "And these monies will be delivered to me within the week. It is a small sum considering what you paid to build Sepphoris."

"And if I refuse?" Tullus could see the anger rising in Chuza's face. He was trapped.

"Gladly refuse. And word of a dangerous, corrupt steward will be known from here to Sepphoris. You must decide, Chuza," and here Appius spoke slowly, "you must decide if you are a friend of Caesar. Declare yourself. And I will convey your word widely."

When the elders of Capernaum began laying out the groundwork for the building of the synagogue, they thought they were living in a dream. Appius delivered the funding he promised

FRIEND OF CAESAR (AMICUS CAESARIS)

When Appius threatens Chuza with this term, he is employing a severe tactic that had a long Greek and Roman history.

For the Romans *friendship* was not a casual term. They discussed it at great length (Latin *amicitia*; Greek *philia*) and wrote about it extensively. The famous Roman poet Martial satirized it for the emperor whose only friends viewed friendship as benefit (*Discourses* 5.19). But the great orator Marcus Tullius Cicero produced an entire book on it (*De Amicitia*) in which he explores and profiles his own experiences with *amicitia* and sees it as one of the greatest virtues. We even have four hundred letters of Cicero to his lifelong friend, Atticus, that spanned their childhood to Cicero's death in 43 B.C., and this provides a direct window into the lived virtue. Cicero's famous *On Old Age* (*De Senectute,* 44 B.C.) was dedicated to his friend Atticus at the end of their lives.

Amicitia could refer to personal affection or sentiment (as in modern use), but usually it referred to something more: alliances, patron/client relations, or deep loyalty. This concept of friendship as loyalty may be behind Jesus' words in John 15:13-15. Jesus is reframing his relationship with his followers in terms they would have recognized: He was their lord to whom they had pledged ultimate allegiance. They would not betray one another.

But this is not Appius's interest with Chuza. His use is specialized and political. "Friend of Caesar" (Latin *amicus*

Caesaris or *amicus Augusti*) was an important political term that began in the Hellenistic period to identify those with trustworthy loyalty to the state or its ruler. The Romans developed it into a technical term to identify either states or people who were allies to Rome (*Amici populi Romani*).

Loss of this title was serious and considered the same as condemnation as a criminal. It meant that one stood against the will of Rome and thus was subversive. In the reign of Tiberius we know of a number of Romans whose careers ended tragically when they were claimed to be "unpatriotic."

This sort of political leverage is seen clearly in John 19:12, when the Jewish leaders threaten Pilate by saying, "If you let this man go, you are no friend of Caesar. Anyone who claims to be a king opposes Caesar." Essentially they are threatening to ruin Pilate's career by reporting his disloyalty to Rome.

but declined to reveal all its sources. Chuza's money had been delivered promptly by one of his servants, and when it was in hand, Appius dismissed him promptly. As far as the elders knew, this gift was something that emerged from Appius's own purse. From Appius's vantage, it was his opportunity to win honor in the eyes of the people he had come to control.

Soon stonecutters from throughout the area began migrating to Capernaum to lend a hand in the work and earn what they could. They carved the foundation blocks from the black basalt stone found naturally throughout the northern coastline. Each of Capernaum's homes was built from it, but now they had the money to cut larger blocks that would support something they thought would be monumental, at least from the perspective of the fishing village. The rubble from abandoned houses was leveled in the center of the village, and a stone-and-dirt platform was built. This was the base on which enormous blocks of basalt were hauled into place for the floor of the prayer hall.

Tullus and Appius were both amazed at how rapidly this project changed the atmosphere of Capernaum. It was a project, a shared

Figure 9.2. Remains of homes at Capernaum

project, money was flowing freely to workers, and excitement was in the air. New optimism swept over Capernaum. Nevertheless, whenever they neared the building site—and Tobias was present, as he always seemed to be—the elder intercepted them. His intentions could hardly be missed. They were Gentiles, and this was to be a building dedicated to God. It seemed foolish and ironic to Appius. Here he was, paying for a building to benefit the Jews, and Tobias was doing his best to keep him away from it.

One afternoon Mariam, watching Tobias perform the same

tired ritual with Appius, called him over. Mariam was not known for wasting time.

"So you'll accept a Gentile's money, but you won't let him see what he's bought?"

Tobias blinked. "We want our prayer hall to bless God, don't we?"

"And God won't be blessed if other people pray in it?"

"The Scripture tells us that when Nehemiah rebuilt the temple he had to separate himself from foreigners. We are building our synagogue. Should it be less holy?"

Mariam, as if she'd been waiting a lifetime to recite a verse to Tobias, said, "But didn't Moses tell us: 'When foreigners reside among you in your land, do not mistreat them. The foreigners residing among you must be treated as your native-born. Love them as yourself, for you were foreigners in Egypt. I am the LORD your God.'"

Tobias was barely amused. "But those Gentiles had to obey the law. Does God neglect his law for Gentiles and require it of us?"

Mariam's frustration peaked. "And what about those of us who lived before Moses? Did God reject Abraham? He wasn't even circumcised, and God was with him! At least you could treat Appius like Abraham treated Melchizedek."

Stalemate. This is how it often ended with Tobias and Mariam, old friends that they were. In the end, neither of them ever felt satisfied.

Appius understood the boundaries that most of the Jews enforced between him and their world. He never entered their homes, and he never invited them to enter his. He watched from a distance. And while he felt that good progress had been made in Capernaum, still, he wondered what would become of his relationship with Chuza. The man believed that this village was his personal resource, not just for Antipas's tax burden but for his own profit as well. And this synagogue represented his loss

MARIAM VERSUS TOBIAS

The conversation that Mariam and Tobias have centers on the appropriate relationship between Judaism and the Gentile world. Progressive Jews, particularly those who lived in the greater Diaspora, were comfortable with Gentile contact. Others who were more conservative insisted on separation and pursued ritual purity intensely. The debate circled around questions of the preservation of racial purity and the importance of Jewish election and its exceptionalism.

But the question remained: How could Israel be a light to the nations when it prohibited any contact with those nations? The temple in Jerusalem became a flashpoint in this debate. Should Gentiles be permitted to enter it and participate in its ceremonies and sacrifices? In the first century, conservatives succeeded in having a wall built in the temple, limiting access to Gentiles. But Jesus found this sort of exclusion offensive. In his temple cleansing he remarked, "Is it not written, 'My house shall be called a house of prayer for all the nations'? But you have made it a den of robbers." Here Jesus is in Mariam's camp, arguing for inclusivity and welcome to Gentiles or "all nations."

In this exchange Mariam and Tobias are citing familiar texts from the Old Testament. Tobias's first volley is likely an echo of Nehemiah 9:2. Miriam cites in response Leviticus 19:33-34. The reference to Melchizedek comes from Genesis 14.

THE CAPERNAUM SYNAGOGUE

Visitors to Capernaum today can see a white limestone synagogue at the center of the excavated village. This white synagogue is likely from the fourth century A.D. However, beneath its floor is a foundation of black basalt, the native building material of this region. Basalt is produced by volcanic activity, and the entire region of Galilee for hundreds of miles has evidence of ancient lava flows.

Figure 9.3. Remains of the fourth-century synagogue at Caesarea

Scholars are convinced that this basalt layer is the foundation of the original synagogue, perhaps from the first century. An excavation begun in the 1960s uncovered the perimeter around the fourth-century synagogue and opened the main floor in the central prayer hall. The earlier basalt foundation is clearly visible on the east exterior of the white synagogue. Beneath the basalt, scholars have found home debris from the Hellenistic era: stairs, waterways and walls. (An example of a basalt synagogue from the fourth century can be found in nearby Chorazin, just north of Capernaum.)

It was in Capernaum's basalt synagogue that Jesus completed his first exorcism (Mk 2:1-12). Luke tells us that the

Figure 9.4. First-century black basalt foundation of the synagogue at Caesarea

centurion of Capernaum paid for its construction (Lk 7:5). But no doubt the Jews of Capernaum had a place of meeting that they used before this. Wherever they met, it would have been called a synagogue.

of face, his dishonor and, above all, his loss of money. Appius wondered whether Chuza would let this pass so easily.

Appius and Tullus were walking near the site at dusk one day to check its progress. Work was being done skillfully, even though the stone, they thought, was too porous and too dark. It was almost black. *They have to plaster these rooms,* Tullus thought. *Otherwise it will be a cave. Or a tomb.*

And then it happened—not far from Appius's villa, near a narrow street darkened by the sunset. Three men who were clearly Jewish rebels had been waiting for them in the darkness.

One man charged quickly, running at them with his sword extended. Appius was wearing his armor but little else that would serve for defense. He carried a gladius at all times strapped to his left hip. Tullus had nothing.

Appius pulled his sword instinctively, and the clash of steel was deafening. Tullus ran behind Appius as the centurion held his ground at the opening of the lane. The skill of this swordsman was astonishing.

Without a shield in his left hand, Appius's sword was his only defense, and he kept it forward constantly. However, his opponent kept pressing on his left, forcing him to brace with his backhand. Appius could not move the combat to his strong right side, and his opponent seemed to know his advantage as he rotated around to Appius's weak flank. For one moment, Appius seemed shaken. But then he stirred to greater action.

The rebel stepped back, took a deep breath and raised his sword with two hands above his head. He was aiming at the left side of Appius's neck and swung the sword explosively. Appius saw it coming and knew it was meant it as a final blow. He crossed his gladius to his left to meet it and attempted to strengthen his defense with his left hand on the hilt. But as he raised his sword with both hands, pain screamed from his damaged shoulder, and he lost his grip. The enemy's sword hit Appius's gladius, but the centurion could not absorb it. The blow cut into him and threw him back as he fell to the ground. He was dazed by the power of the hit and knew he was wounded.

The other two attackers were now free to enter the fray, and the three of them now stood facing Tullus. They paused, knowing this would be no fight. The leader looked at Appius, who was struggling to regain his feet. But clearly the centurion was compromised. Then Tullus made a sudden move toward Appius's fallen sword—a foolish and impulsive gesture—which the rebel answered with a sudden thrust of his own sword. The blade found Tullus completely unprepared, and as it sunk into his belly, Tullus looked down with horror. As the rebel withdrew the thrust, a savage pain shot through Tullus's body. He covered himself with his hands and fell to his knees.

The rebel now turned to Appius, who was in no condition to repulse the men. But denying this final reality—that he had lost, that his fate was now set—he prepared to launch an assault even as he heard the men laughing over him.

At that moment Appius heard a sound that echoed from his entire career in Legion Gallica: the sound of running behind him, and the grunt of an infantryman launching a javelin with enormous velocity. The spear ripped through the air just over Appius's head and found its mark in the rebel leader. Shock swept over the man as the weapon flew through him cleanly and hit the stone wall behind him. Sparks sprayed in the darkness.

It was Marcus. His gladius was drawn, and letting out a battle scream, he drove in full sprint toward the other two, who quickly fled into the darkness of the night.

Marcus stopped to check on Appius and brought him to his feet. Seeing that the rebel leader was dead, they turned to Tullus, who was bleeding and unconscious. Men came running from the villa, and Tullus was quickly hoisted into strong arms and carried home.

Appius was furious. Utterly furious. He was ready to march directly to Sepphoris and kill Chuza and his entire family. Appius's trust in the village of Capernaum had evaporated in an instant.

Marcus and Appius walked to the fallen rebel and flipped him on his back. They looked closely at the man's still-open eyes. In the fading light they recognized him. This wasn't a delegation from Chuza. These men weren't even Jewish.

It was Axius of Carthage, the tribune's guard from the Caesarea gatehouse.

10

One Week in Capernaum

The violence of the attack near Appius's villa was utterly unexpected. This was to be a joyous week that celebrated the construction of the synagogue and stronger alliances with the Jewish leaders. All was going well. But the week now had become a disaster—an unmitigated disaster. Fear and anger would poison every relationship in Capernaum. Even the elders worried that the congenial Appius was lost to them.

But it would turn out to be something more. It would be a week no one would forget.

Appius refused to have his own wounds tended and became hardened and resolute. He was not sure what to do: he wanted to attack someone somewhere—that was his instinct—but he had no outlet for his rage and his confusion. Anger was brimming inside him, and anyone might be his target. Most in the villa kept their distance.

Tullus's wound was small but deep. The cut barely betrayed any damage to the young man's body, but everyone knew this was serious. Gaius sent a guard at once to find Mariam or her husband to see what could be done. Mariam immediately ran to the villa and stayed at Tullus's side late into the night. Livia assisted and conveyed supplies as they were needed. The sword had pierced deep, wreaking its damage within, and now there was a spreading darkness around the cut. Mariam was able to close the wound and apply herb poultices, but she was not confident they could save him. She prayed for Tullus fervently. But he was delirious and unable to respond to anything they asked.

Appius refused to let even Mariam look at his own wounds and paced the villa in his distress over what had happened. He also refused to change his tunic, wearing the blood of the attack as a reminder of what had been done. He wanted to send for a physician in Legion Gallica, but he knew the tribunes would never release one of their physicians to travel the distance to help a slave.

Appius blamed himself. He had never before lost a private battle like this. But the incident sobered him: his damaged shoulder genuinely compromised his ability to defend himself. And it made him feel incompetent. He would never have lost—he would never have abandoned Tullus—had he been himself. He could not let go of his final memory on the street: Tullus's fear, his sudden move and his shock when he was felled. All this happened as Appius lay on his back looking on in agony at what transpired beyond his reach. Only Appius knew that when Tullus collapsed their eyes were fastened on each other.

Mariam left in the middle of the night but returned before sunrise and was met by Livia and Gaius. Both looked tired and shattered. Mariam barely paused to greet them.

"How is he, Livia? Signs of change?"

"He sleeps a sleep unlike any I've seen before. I cannot awaken him. And then suddenly he is with me again."

"And the wound?"

"It grows worse, I fear. The color grows. And it shows no sign of improving."

"Soon it will grow rank unless we open it and remove the blood."

"And he has fever, Mariam. He is wet with sweat and is in constant pain."

"Take me to him. I must see our young Tullus before he leaves us."

Together the women made their way to the room that had been set aside for Tullus the night before. Livia's report was accurate, and the visit confirmed Mariam's worst fears. She knelt beside Tullus's bed and placed her hand gently on his forehead. Heat radiated from his skin. She whispered to him, "Hold on, Tullus. Hold on my son. God has not abandoned you. *You are not lost.*"

Mariam stood and whispered, "He is in serious danger, Livia. We will know within the week. Few can survive a wound like this. The fever will grow and consume him. Tullus is in the hands of his God now."

"His God?" Livia caught Mariam's words. It sounded out of place.

"Yes. If you must know, Tullus is one of us. He belongs to the God of Abraham. And with us he has begun to reclaim the faith of his fathers. Tobias has been meeting with him. But you must tell no one."

Livia stood silently, thinking. It was a secret not even she had known. And it made Tullus even more endearing to her—that this man lived with something he could tell no Roman. But it also gave her some assurance.

With Tullus asleep and breathing in shallow gasps, Mariam took Livia by the arm and walked out into the courtyard. The sun was just rising. "There is only one hope for him, Livia. We must find a healer who is stronger than this evil. We cannot repair what we see here."

"Asclepius? We need a priest of Asclepius," Livia offered.

THE NAZARENE HEALER

Jesus had a number of popular names during his lifetime. One was the "Nazarene" (Mk 14:67), because he had come from Nazareth, a village southwest of Capernaum in the foothills of southern Galilee. Jesus grew up in Nazareth, and it was in the Nazareth synagogue that he announced publicly for the first time his identity as the Messiah of Israel (Lk 4:16-30). After reading some of the most important messianic texts from the Hebrew Scriptures in Isaiah, Jesus remarked, "Today this scripture has been fulfilled in your hearing." This announcement did not present a problem per se, but then Jesus went on to define his messianic mission by telling two stories, one about Elijah and another about Elisha (1 Kings 17; 2 Kings 5). In each case, due to the faithlessness of Israel, God had sent messengers to Gentiles and blessed them. The implication was clear: if Jesus' own ministry was met with unfaithfulness, he too would follow Elijah and Elisha and expand the work of his kingdom to include Gentiles. This notion was met with outrage, and the synagogue crowd tried to kill him (Lk 4:29).

Even though Jesus grew up in Nazareth, following this dangerous conflict in the Nazareth synagogue he left there and came to Capernaum (Mt 4:13; Lk 4:31). In Capernaum the village commonly understood that when he stayed with them, he was "home" (Mk 2:1).

But Jesus was also known as a healer. Even among skeptical scholars there is broad agreement that, despite what one may believe about miracles today, certainly in Jesus' own day he was well known as a miracle worker and healer. The evidence appears in every stratum of the Gospel tradition (Q, Mark, John, and narratives unique to Luke and Matthew). He also cited Isaiah (Mt 11:5; Lk 7:22; cf. Lk 4:18) to explain that healing was essential to his work: "Go back and report to John what you have seen and heard: The blind receive sight, the lame walk, those who have leprosy are cleansed, the deaf hear, the dead are raised, and the good news is proclaimed to the poor." His popularity as a healer was so widespread that it frequently became a problem with the crowds who sought him out. Mark reports, "Because of the crowd he told his disciples to have a small boat ready for him, to keep the people from crowding him. For he had healed many, so that those with diseases were pushing forward to touch him" (Mk 3:9-10).

"No, my dear." Mariam resisted frustration. "We need a prophet-healer who can bring the power of Tullus's God to his aid." Mariam continued walking and then paused.

"We need to find the healer of Nazareth."

"That man the authorities are watching? The man Antipas hates? The one Rome is worried about? Are you serious? This may bring us worse problems."

"We need to bring the Nazarene, for he alone knows what to do."

"How can you be sure? Should we talk to Tobias? Maybe Appius should know."

"I'd rather talk about it with Appius than Tobias. But it doesn't matter. We either get what we need or we lose Tullus.

It's that simple." It was clear that Mariam was not going to be dissuaded. She drew Livia close and whispered, "I know him. I know this Nazarene."

"You know him?"

"My family knows him. Some are followers. Once he healed me as well. This is why I believe he can help Tullus."

"But how can you find him? And how quickly?"

"We must send a messenger. He has other followers in the village, and we can send one of them. But we must keep this quiet. If he comes, we don't want him to be greeted by Antipas's police." Mariam was already working out the logistics in her mind, and Livia was privy to very little of it. It was time for her to leave, and Livia knew it. Mariam sped from the villa and headed into the village.

Antipas had agents who worked for him in the village, creating registers of property for taxation. Mariam contacted one of them, named Levi, and gave him a firm order. Levi was also a follower of the Nazarene and would be sympathetic. He was to travel directly to Sepphoris, to the tax offices of Antipas. But he should look for Joanna, Chuza's wife, and tell her to send the message. She too was a follower of the Nazarene. "Tell her that Capernaum needs him immediately. That it is Mariam who asks for him. Tell him that we have prayed but that we are at our end."

Levi knew there was no discussing this plan, and he left at once. News of the attack on the centurion had now spread throughout the village. And the tragedy of this was compounded when they thought about the building of the synagogue. *Will the centurion now become an enemy? Will he suspect us?* Appius had the body of Axius quickly removed in the night. He did not want anyone to think there were divisions in the ranks of the Romans. This might inspire yet more hostilities of a different sort. He ordered his men to build a pyre, and they burned it outside the soldiers' camp. Some desecrated Axius's body before they finished with it. It needed to be dishonored on behalf of Appius and his household.

When she had done all she could, Mariam returned to the villa. Now to wait. Levi was on the road to Sepphoris, and Mariam had resolved to sit with Tullus until this had reached its conclusion. Livia sat with her. At about midday Livia heard what she thought was the most mysterious, magical singing she could remember. Mariam began to sing in Hebrew. As she sang, she draped her arms over Tullus's still body. As Livia would later learn, it was a song of lament, a Jewish song, reserved for those who were facing the tragedy of their own death.

My God, my God, why have you forsaken me?
Why are you so far from saving me,
so far from the words of my groaning?
My God, I cry out by day, but you do not answer,
by night, but I find no rest.
Yet you are enthroned as the Holy One;
you are the praise of Israel.
In you our ancestors put their trust;
they trusted and you delivered them.
They cried to you and were saved;
in you they trusted and were not disappointed.
Yet you brought me out of the womb;
you made me feel secure on my mother's breast.
From birth I was cast on you;
from my mother's womb you have been my God.
Do not be far from me,
for trouble is near and there is no one to help.
But I am a worm, not a human being;
I am scorned by everyone, despised by the people.

All who see me mock me;
they hurl insults, shaking their heads.
"He trusts in the LORD,*" they say,*
"let the LORD *rescue him.*
Let him deliver him,
since he delights in him."
But you, LORD, *do not be far from me.*
You are my strength; come quickly to help me.

Mariam paused and moved her hands gently over the festering wound, covered with linen bandages. She looked at Tullus's face, then back to the wound, and continued.

Deliver me from the sword,
my precious life from the power of the dogs.
Rescue me from the mouth of the lions;
save me from the horns of the wild oxen.
I will declare your name to my people;
in the assembly I will praise you.
You who fear the LORD, *praise him!*
All you descendants of Jacob, honor him!
Revere him,
all you descendants of Israel!
For he has not despised or scorned
the suffering of the afflicted one;
he has not hidden his face from him
but has listened to his cry for help.

Livia was struck by the passion of this prayer—for obviously it was a prayer—and through it and through Mariam's gestures, she knew how deeply this woman had come to care for Tullus. She was calling her god in her own language. Livia understood this, and she stepped back and listened with curiosity and respect.

Appius was hovering near the door with Marcus and Gaius. Livia went out to join them.

MARIAM'S LAMENT

Mariam is using her memory of Psalm 22. This psalm was often a deathbed psalm in Judaism and was likely recited in its entirety on the cross by Jesus ("My God, My God, why have you forsaken me" [Mk 15:34]). The psalm begins with a sorrowful lament but evolves quickly into a psalm of faith and confidence.

"What is happening? What does Mariam think we should do?" Appius asked. It had been a very hard season for both Appius and Livia. The loss of the pregnancy was bad enough. Now Mariam was tending yet another, even more severe, tragedy in the household.

"We are waiting. Waiting to see whether the Jewish god will act as Asclepius helped you, Appius. But Mariam has also sent a messenger to bring a Jewish healer."

"Who is this? And why did I not know?"

"Do you really think Mariam would have asked you? And if you said no—seriously Appius—would this have changed anything? It is a healer from Nazareth."

"The prophet-healer from Nazareth? The man who talks about his kingdom? The ally with the Baptist that Herod Antipas killed? Why should we welcome *him* to this village?"

"It is the same man. And so we must keep this quiet, she says. He is powerful. And he is our only hope. We must choose to take this risk or lose Tullus. But Mariam says he is harmless. Antipas hates anyone who has a following larger than his."

"His name? What's his name?" Appius pressed.

"I asked Mariam. He is Yeshua bar Yosef. But he has now left Nazareth. And when he stays anywhere for long, he prefers to live in Capernaum. They say he is a great healer."

"Then we wait," Appius said. "Let us wait and see if this Yeshua bar Yosef appears."

When Levi returned two days later, Tullus's condition had

JESUS (YESHUA BAR YOSEF)

In first-century Jewish communities, a man would ordinarily have a given name that was then further defined by reference to his father or his village. Jesus was thus "Joseph's son" (Lk 4:22), or he might be "Jesus of Nazareth" (Mk 10:47), or "Jesus the prophet of Nazareth" (Mt 21:11). "Jesus Christ" was a title of faith used later by believers, confessing that "Jesus is the Messiah" (*Christ* is a Greek form of the Hebrew word for "messiah").

However, the actual name "Jesus" was never used. This is an English form that derives from the Greek (*Iesous*) and Latin (*Iesus*). Semitic languages like Aramaic and Hebrew did not use the "j" sound. His name in Aramaic was *Yeshua* (Hebrew *Yehoshua*), which stems from the Old Testament name Joshua (Hebrew meaning, "Yahweh saves"). In the Greek Old Testament (the Septuagint) the Hebrew *Yehoshua* is always translated into Greek as *Iesous*.

Aramaic speakers generally knew Jesus as "Yeshua bar Yosef" (Jesus son of Joseph).

worsened. His death was imminent. But Levi's report to Mariam was encouraging. Joanna knew exactly where Yeshua was, and she had sent a slave to get word to him immediately. The village should expect him very soon.

Mariam found Tobias and decided she needed to prepare the elders for what was to come. She did not want them to be surprised. She found them at the site of the synagogue.

"I have sent a messenger to Yeshua of Nazareth. And he has promised to come to help Tullus," Mariam said. "He is a great healer and will know what to do." Tobias was equally worried. He too was committed to Tullus and his newly found faith. He would either welcome the healer or, if all failed, begin to plan how he might plan a Jewish funeral for Tullus, which he knew Appius might not receive well.

"When will he arrive?"

"The promise is for tomorrow. And we must pray that Tullus will survive until then."

"But we have a problem. We cannot ask Yeshua to enter this Gentile household. He is a holy man, and that would make him unclean. You would not ask this of me, nor can we ask this of him."

"But I *would* ask this of you, Tobias. These rules are like a mountain hanging by a thread. Tullus cannot be moved. It would kill him. And the healer must go to him. Let Yeshua decide whether he wants to enter the Roman house."

"Perhaps it is God's will that Tullus's life is ended," Tobias brooded. "Perhaps we should wait and see what happens. God alone assigns our days."

"Perhaps. But you do not know God's will. No one knows that. Therefore we do all we can to save him." Then Mariam considered a different approach. "But you are forgetting about Appius in this, Tobias. You want him to be good to us, as he has already. So he has asked me to request something of you. *Will you be the one who asks the Nazarene to tend to his servant?* That is all he asks, and it is very little. You lead our community. You alone can do this."

"I will make this request. But you must think of a way to bring Tullus to him. I will not ask Yeshua to enter the centurion's villa."

At about noon the next day it was the children playing in the street who saw him first. Tobias had assigned them that morning to watch the road from the west, the road that led from Gennesaret. When they spotted him coming, they ran to Tobias's home and alerted him. Tobias's wife was already preparing a splendid afternoon meal with her servants. The other elders were ready as well. There would be a meal soon after Yeshua arrived.

More than a dozen boys under the age of ten were racing through the village directly for Tobias's gate. As soon as they had told Tobias the news, the boys raced back again to the edge of the village. They knew Yeshua bar Yosef from his previous visits. He always stopped for them, and sometimes he played with them. They sensed he liked them. And he knew their names.

Yeshua was traveling with his growing band of followers. They looked no different than every other peasant in these hills: tired, hungry and lean from hard travel and labor. But it was clear that Yeshua was leading them.

As he entered Capernaum, the boys immediately swarmed him. Up the street he could see Tobias and the elders ready to greet him formally. But still, he stopped, knelt down and talked with the children. Many of their parents belonged to his followers.

In a few minutes he reached Tobias, who offered his first words. He was arrayed in his finest robe, as were the other elders of the community who stood nearby. Tobias greeted Yeshua generously with two kisses on behalf of the village and told him that preparations were made for him to share a meal with him and the elders at his own villa.

"But we would ask one favor of you. We are now a Roman garrison town. We have soldiers camped nearby and a centurion who oversees everything. He is a good man. He loves our people, and he has built our synagogue. But he has a servant who is dear to him that is very ill, near to death in fact. He needs your help." Tobias knew he had to make this request. The entire village knew Tullus's condition and Appius's commitment to him. And they knew why Yeshua was there.

Tobias led him in the general direction of Appius's villa, hoping against hope that Mariam had come up with some plan, some way to make this happen. He did not tell Yeshua that he was going to a Gentile household, only that they were going to the servant's bedside.

But before they arrived, Gaius met them on the road. Behind him, not far away, standing before his gate, Appius was in plain view. He was watching Gaius, waiting to see the results of a message he had sent. Appius understood his place: he was not only a Gentile but a Roman, the occupier and enemy. He was the very opposite of this Jewish holy man. He did not believe in this man's kingdom and doubted whether this Nazarene believed in Rome's kingdom. They were men standing on opposite sides of a major disagreement.

Gaius announced, glancing back at the villa, that he had a message from Appius. He spoke directly to Yeshua. "Lord, do not trouble yourself. I am not worthy to have you come under my roof. Therefore I did not presume to come to you."

Appius accepted the barriers that would keep this man from entering a Gentile household. If it seemed impossible for Tobias, it certainly was impossible for the healer Yeshua.

Gaius continued Appius's message: "Say the word, and my servant will be healed. For I too am a man set under authority, with soldiers under me: and I say to one, 'Go,' and he goes; and to another, 'Come,' and he comes; and to my servant, 'Do this,' and he does it."

Tobias was astounded. Even Appius was maintaining the boundary. Even he was keeping the healer away from Tullus. Now, if Tobias enforced the boundary, Mariam and others could hardly blame him.

When Yeshua heard these things, he too was amazed. Turning to Tobias and the crowd that had gathered, he said, "I tell you. Not even in Israel have I found faith like this."

Tobias was stunned at the affront to the Jewish people. The grumbling on the street among the elders was audible, and Yeshua ignored it. He then looked beyond Gaius and spoke in a voice now aimed at Appius. "Let it be done for you as you have believed."

Appius did not know what he believed. He held more hope than belief. He knew that Mariam believed, and he was willing to act on the faith of someone he trusted. Appius stood motionless on the step before his villa's gate. He simply looked at this man and wondered whether he could be serious. Appius had seen the great healing centers of Asclepius and the intricate healing ceremonies of his priests. His belief—or what little he had—slowly began to evaporate. A Jewish peasant in a remote little fishing village would not be able to do what Asclepius sometimes could not do.

Appius turned and walked back into the villa, unsure of what to do next. He was filled with questions and apprehension. He had hoped against hope. But skepticism continued to haunt his thoughts.

Just then Appius heard a cry from an inner room. Mariam and Livia were inside with Tullus. The midwife stepped into the courtyard and called out. Appius came at a run, fearing the worst. That Tullus had died, that hope would again be ruined, that life would always rob one of the joys one treasured. Appius had seen a lot of this. He desired to see no more. His doubts about the Nazarene were being realized. It was, after all, a foolish quest for hope.

When he arrived, Mariam pulled him into the room. Tullus was sitting on the edge of his bed, weak but vital. Livia was laughing and crying, overcome with tears, and fervently hugging Tullus. Appius wondered whether she might hurt the boy. But

Figure 10.1. Reproduction of a Roman villa's garden at the Getty Villa near Los Angeles

Tullus looked up, and for the first time since the attack, he gazed directly at Appius, recognized him and tried to speak. Appius couldn't believe what he was seeing.

Mariam stood nearby, smiling, her arms folded. "Someone needs to get this boy something to eat."

For minutes Appius was in a daze. He found it impossible to take in everything that had transpired in this week. His rage at Axium was matched now by his joy at seeing Tullus sitting, standing, even walking in his room. When Appius walked into the courtyard, however, he was unprepared for what came next.

Yeshua the healer was standing alone within his open gate. Appius did not know whether he should approach or stay away. It didn't matter. Yeshua was walking toward him.

Yeshua entered the courtyard filled with statues of Apollo and ignored them. But he stopped when he came to the sculpture of the deer and the dogs. He looked at it for what seemed like minutes, in silence. Then he reached up and brushed the face of the deer with his hand. His eyes said everything. He then looked at Appius with a prolonged gaze. And at that moment—he could never explain why—Appius resolved to remove the sculpture and destroy it.

"Walk with me."

Appius knew it was an order and that it was one he wished to obey. They entered the new garden next to the courtyard, now

Figure 10.2. Close-up of the deer and dogs sculpture

just coming to life with the flourishing greenery of its new plants and herbs. A summer clematis had climbed one of the statues of Apollo and was already beginning to display its deep purple flowers. There were bright red flowers that always grew wild in the Galilee hillsides. The sun was shining, and a young pomegranate tree was offering its first red blossoms.

Figure 10.3. A flowering clematis

Yeshua sat on the rim of the new garden fountain, cupped some of its water and took a drink. He looked at Appius patiently.

"You are a good man, Appius. But you are also broken. It remains to be seen which is broken more, your body or your heart. Please tell me."

These words were like another arrow fired from an unexpected quarter. They were a piercing echo of words spoken by a tribune in Raphana long ago.

"My body was broken. . . ."

"At Dura. I know this. I can heal all of you, if you wish."

Appius felt fear rising within. He rarely felt afraid. But this man unnerved him. And hope . . . it made him anxious, because it could so easily be stripped away.

"Step nearer, friend of my people." Yeshua stood, then placed his right hand on Appius's left shoulder, closed his eyes and spoke words, Hebrew words that he never explained. In an instant—he could never describe how he knew this—Appius knew that he had been healed as a radiant warmth shot through his body. Appius cautiously raised his left arm beyond the reach he had known for some time. It had been restored. There was no pain. Strength had returned. And Appius's eyes welled with tears.

"This is a gift to you, Appius of Attalia, not from Apollo but from the God of Israel. He is a living God, a God of power and of healing. Apollo is an imagined god, or perhaps he is as you once imagined yourself. You must learn these things. And you must unlearn many other things you believe to be true."

Appius noticed that Mariam, Tullus and Livia had joined them in the garden. They were approaching hesitantly, cautiously. . . . They knew that Yeshua was talking with Appius, and they could see the centurion wiping tears from his eyes, something Livia had never seen in her many years with him in Gallica. She began to go to him, but Mariam held her arm. Something was happening in this garden, and it was between Yeshua and Appius. It must not be interrupted. Livia would find her moment later.

Minutes passed before Yeshua looked at Mariam, smiled at her and said, "This has been a good day, Mariam. Today we have created two new men. I think we ought to have a banquet right here in Appius's villa."

Mariam liked this. She nodded and went to find Gaius.

THE CENTURION OF CAPERNAUM

The story of the centurion of Capernaum is recorded in Matthew 8:5-13 and Luke 7:1-10. Scholars assume that these stories have been abbreviated and so they do not supply us with all of their details. In some cases, important things are left out. Matthew (who tends to prefer shorter accounts) has the centurion ask for the healing himself. Luke (who underscores the differences between Jew and Gentile) supplies further information. Luke says the centurion first sent Jewish elders to intercept Jesus and inquire about healing the centurion's slave. But before they arrived the centurion then sent someone else, who asked for the healing from a distance, thus protecting Jesus from the impurity of stepping into a Gentile home.

Figure 10.4. A proud centurion

Either way, the slave (who is the focus of the story) is *at the point of death* when Jesus heals him. Matthew adds that he is paralyzed and in terrible pain. The Gospels do not say what exactly is wrong with the servant, but they agree that he was healed from a distance with Jesus' word. The story of the centurion and his servant ends with a dramatic healing, but we are given no further explanations or any continuing narrative. But surely there was more to the story.

Of course the final meeting of Appius and Jesus is fictional. It borrows motifs from other Gospel stories and from themes in the Old Testament. It is likely, however, that Jesus would have further contact with the centurion, who lived in this small town that Jesus called home. It would make sense that Jesus knew his name, the name of his servant and members of his familia.

Maps of Galilee and Syria

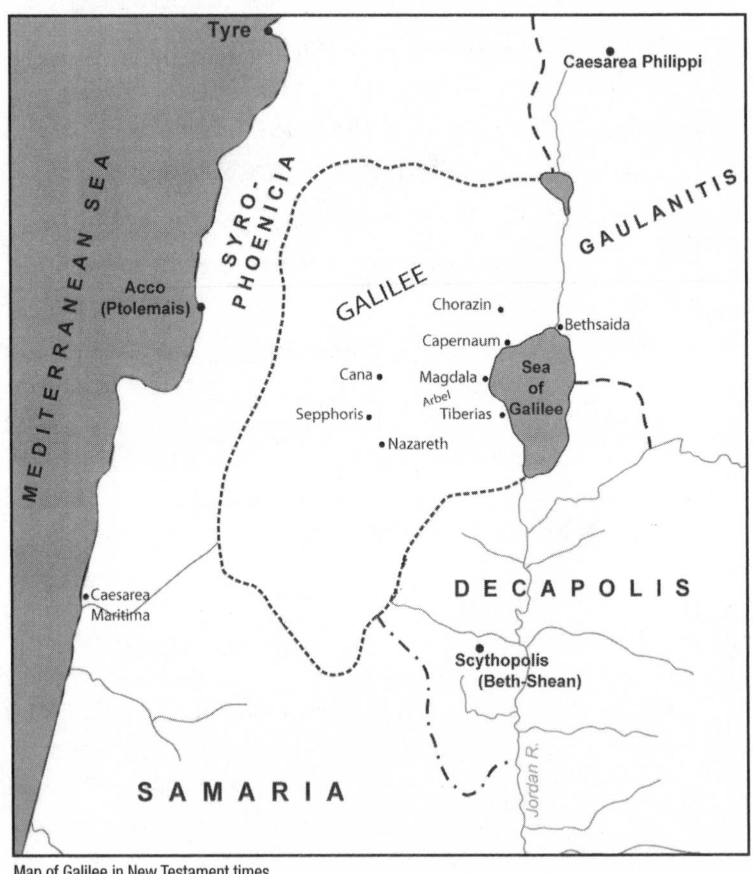

Map of Galilee in New Testament times

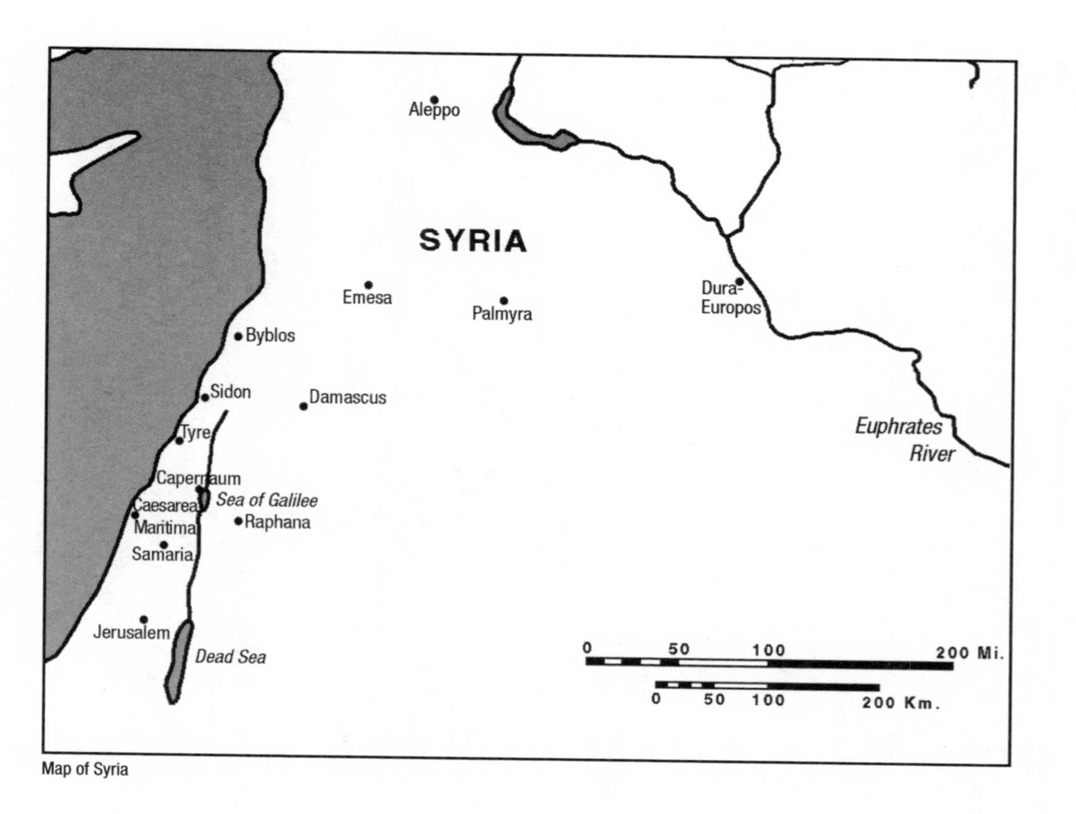

Aleppo
SYRIA
Emesa
Palmyra
Dura-
Europos
Byblos
Sidon
Damascus
Tyre
Euphrates
River
Capernaum
Sea of Galilee
Caesarea
Maritima
Raphana
Samaria
Jerusalem
Dead Sea
0
50
100
200 Mi.
0
50
100
200 Km.

Map of Syria

Image Credits and Permissions

Figure 1.1. Kim Walton. Altes Museum, Berlin
Figure 1.2. Kim Walton. Altes Museum, Berlin
Figure 1.3. Kim Walton. Palatine Museum, Rome
Figure 1.4. © Ritmeyer Archaeological Design
Figure 2.1. © barbulat / Fotolia.com
Figure 2.2. Ted Chi / Wikimedia Commons
Figure 2.3. De Agostini Picture Library / G. Dagli Orti / Bridgeman Images
Figure 2.4. © Bbbar / Dreamstime.com - Site Of Palmyra Photo
Figure 3.1. William L. Krewson / BiblePlaces.com
Figure 3.2. Baker Photo Archive. The British Museum
Figure 3.3. Baker Photo Archive. The British Museum
Figure 3.4. Baker Photo Archive. The British Museum
Figure 3.5. Baker Photo Archive
Figure 3.6. Kim Walton. The Louvre
Figure 4.1. Baker Photo Archive
Figure 4.2. Kim Walton
Figure 4.3. Kim Walton. The British Museum
Figure 4.4. Kim Walton
Figure 4.5. © Ca2hill / Dreamstime.com - Stone Bed in Pompeii Photo
Figure 5.1. Baker Photo Archive. The Eretz Israel Museum
Figure 5.2. Marie-Lan Nguyen. The Louvre / Wikimedia Commons
Figure 5.3. Kim Walton. The Altes Museum, Berlin
Figure 5.4. Museo Archeologico Nazionale, Naples, Italy / Bridgeman Images
Figure 5.5. Baker Photo Archive
Figure 6.1. Baker Photo Archive
Figure 6.2. Baker Photo Archive
Figure 6.3. Baker Photo Archive
Figure 6.4. Baker Photo Archive
Figure 7.1. De Agostini Picture Library / C. Bevilacqua / Bridgeman Images
Figure 7.2. Kim Walton. Yigal Allon Museum, Kibbutz Ginosar, Israel
Figure 7.3. Herculaneum, Campania, Italy / Giraudon / Bridgeman Images
Figure 7.4. Baker Photo Archive. The British Museum
Figure 8.1. Werner Forman Archive / Bridgeman Images
Figure 8.2. © The Trustees of the British Museum / Art Resource, NY
Figure 8.3. De Agostini Picture Library / R. Pedicini / Bridgeman Images
Figure 8.4. Baker Photo Archive. The Masada Museum
Figure 9.1. Private Collection / Photo © Zev Radovan / Bridgeman Images
Figure 9.2. Kim Walton
Figure 9.3. Kim Walton
Figure 9.4. Kim Walton
Figure 10.1. © Poi80 / Dreamstime.com - Garden in Gettyvilla Photo
Figure 10.2. Herculaneum, Campania, Italy / Giraudon / Bridgeman Images
Figure 10.3. © Turpentinevinegar / Dreamstime.com - Clematis Photo
Figure 10.4. IKAI. Universalmuseum Joanneum, Styria, Austria / Wikimedia Commons